ALMOST IMPOSSIBLE

ALSO BY NICOLE WILLIAMS

Trusting You & Other Lies

ALMOST IMPOSSIBLE

NICOLE WILLIAMS

CROWN   New York

Text copyright © 2018 by Nicole Williams
Cover art copyright © 2018 by Regina Flath

All rights reserved. Published in the United States by Crown Books for Young Readers, an imprint of Random House Children's Books, a division of Penguin Random House LLC, New York.

Crown and the colophon are registered trademarks of Penguin Random House LLC.

Visit us on the Web! GetUnderlined.com

Educators and librarians, for a variety of teaching tools, visit us at RHTeachersLibrarians.com

Library of Congress Cataloging-in-Publication Data is available upon request.
ISBN 978-0-553-49881-3 (trade pbk.) —
ISBN 978-0-553-49883-7 (ebook)

Printed in the United States of America
10 9 8 7 6 5 4 3 2 1
First Edition

Dedicated to you, my dear reader.
You might be one of seven and a half billion, but never
forget that you're one in *seven and a half billion, too.*

ALMOST IMPOSSIBLE

Chapter One

Anything was possible. At least that's what it felt like.

Summer seventeen was going to be one for the record books. I already knew it. I could *feel* it—from the nervous-excited swirl in my stomach to the buzz in the air around me. This was going to be the summer—*my* summer.

"Last chance to cry uncle or forever hold your peace," Mom sang beside me in the backseat of the cab we'd caught at the airport. Her hand managed to tighten around mine even more, cutting off the last bit of my circulation. If there was any left.

I tried to look the precise amount of unsure before answering. "So long, last chance," I said, waving out the window.

Mom sighed, squeezing my hand harder still. It was starting to go numb now. Summer seventeen might find me one hand short if Mom didn't ease up on the death grip.

She and her band, the Shrinking Violets, were going to be touring internationally after finally hitting it big, but she was moping because this was the first summer we wouldn't be together. Actually, it would be the first time we'd been apart ever.

I'd sold her on the idea of me staying in the States with her sister and family by going on about how badly I wanted to experience one summer as a normal, everyday American teenager before graduating from high school. One chance to see what it was like to stay in the same place, with the same people, before I left for college. One last chance to see what life as an American teen was really like.

She bought it . . . *eventually*.

She'd have her bandmates and tens of thousands of adoring fans to keep her company—she could do without me for a couple of months. I hoped.

It had always been just Mom and me from day one. She had me when she was young—like *young* young—and even though her boyfriend pretty much bailed before the line turned pink, she'd done just fine on her own.

We'd both kind of grown up together, and I knew she'd missed out on a lot by raising me. I wanted this to be a summer for the record books for her, too. One she could really live up, not having to worry about taking care of her teenage daughter. Plus, I wanted to give her a chance to experience what life without me would be like. Soon I'd be off to college somewhere, and I figured easing her into the empty-nester phase was a better approach than going cold turkey.

"You packed sunscreen, right?" Mom's bracelets jingled as she leaned to look out her window, staring at the bright blue sky like it was suspect.

"SPF seventy for hot days, fifty for warm days, and thirty for overcast ones." I toed the trusty duffel resting at my feet.

It had traveled the globe with me for the past decade and had the wear to prove it.

"That's my fair-skinned girl." When Mom looked over at me, the crease between her eyebrows carved deeper with worry.

"You might want to check into SPF yourself. You're not going to be in your midthirties forever, you know?"

Mom groaned. "Don't remind me. But I'm already beyond SPF's help at this point. Unless it can help fix a saggy butt and crow's-feet." She pinched invisible wrinkles and wiggled her butt against the seat.

It was my turn to groan. It was annoying enough that people mistook us for sisters all the time, but it was worse that she could (and did) wear the same jeans as me. There should be some rule that moms aren't allowed to takes clothes from the closets of their teenage daughters.

When the cab turned down Providence Avenue, I felt a sudden streak of panic. Not for myself, but for my mom.

Could she survive a summer when I wasn't at her side, reminding her when the cell phone bill was due or updating her calendar so she knew where to be and when to be there? Would she be okay without me reminding her that fruits and vegetables were part of the food pyramid for a reason and making sure everything was all set backstage?

"Hey." Mom gave me a look, her eyes suggesting she could read my thoughts. "I'll be okay. I'm a strong, empowered thirty-four-year-old woman."

"Cell phone charger." I yanked the one dangling from her oversized, metal-studded purse, which I'd wrapped in hot pink tape so it stood out. "I've packed you two extras to get you through the summer. When you get down to your last one, make sure to pick up two more so you're covered—"

"Jade, please," she interrupted. "I've only lost a few. It's not like I've misplaced . . ."

"Thirty-two phone chargers in the past five years?" When she opened her mouth to protest, I added, "I've got the receipts to prove it, too."

Her mouth clamped closed as the cab rolled up to my aunt's house.

"What am I going to do without you?" Mom swallowed, dropping her big black retro sunglasses over her eyes to hide the tears starting to form, to my surprise.

I was better at keeping my emotions hidden, so I didn't dig around in my purse for sunglasses. "Um, I don't know? Maybe rock a sold-out international tour? Six continents in three months? Fifty concerts in ninety days? That kind of thing?"

Mom started to smile. She loved music—writing it, listening to it, playing it—and was a true musician. She hadn't gotten into it to become famous or make the Top 40 or anything like that; she'd done it because it was who she was. She was the same person playing to a dozen people in a crowded café as she was now, the lead singer of one of the biggest bands in the world playing to an arena of thousands.

"Sounds pretty killer. All of those countries. All of that adventure." Mom's hand was on the door handle, but it looked more like she was trying to keep the taxi door closed than to open it. "Sure you don't want to be a part of it?"

I smiled thinly back at my mom, her wild brown hair spilling over giant glasses. She had this boundless sense of adventure—always had and always would—so it was hard for her to comprehend how her own offspring could feel any different.

"Promise to call me every day and send me pictures?" I said, feeling the driver lingering outside my door with luggage in hand. This was it.

Mom exhaled, lifting her pinkie toward me. "Promise."

I curled my pinkie around hers and forced a smile. "Love you, Mom."

Her finger wound around mine as tightly as she had clenched my other hand on the ride here. "Love you no matter what." Then she shoved her door open and crawled out, but not before I noticed one tiny tear escape her sunglasses.

By the time I'd stepped out of the cab, all signs of that tear or any others were gone. Mom did tears as often as she wrote moving love songs. In other words, never.

As she dug around in her purse for her wallet to pay the driver, I took a minute to inspect the house in front of me. The last time we'd been here was for Thanksgiving three years ago. Or was it four? I couldn't remember, but it was long enough to have forgotten how bright white my aunt and uncle's house was, how the windows glowed from being so clean and the landscaping looked almost fake it was so well kept.

It was pretty much the total opposite of the tour buses and extended-stay hotels I'd spent most of my life in. My mother, Meg Abbott, did not do tidy.

"Back zipper pocket," I said as she struggled to find the money in her wallet.

"Aha," she announced, freeing a few bills to hand to the

driver, whose patience was wilting. After taking her luggage, she shouldered up beside me.

"So the neat-freak thing gets worse with time." Mom gaped at the walkway leading up to the cobalt-blue front door, where a Davenport nameplate sparkled in the sunlight. It wasn't an exaggeration to say most of the surfaces I'd eaten off of weren't as clean as the stretch of concrete in front of me.

"Mom . . . ," I warned, when she shuddered after she roamed to inspect the window boxes bursting with scarlet geraniums.

"I'm not being mean," she replied as we started down the walkway. "I'm appreciating my sister's and my differences. That's all."

Right then, the front door whisked open and my aunt seemed to float from it, a measured smile in place, not a single hair out of place.

"Appreciating our differences," Mom muttered under her breath as we moved closer.

I bit my lip to keep from laughing as the two sisters embraced.

Mom had long dark hair and fell just under the average-height bar like me. Aunt Julie, conversely, had light hair she kept swishing above her shoulders, and she was tall and thin. Her eyes were almost as light blue as mine, compared to Mom's, which were almost as dark as her hair.

It wasn't only their physical differences that set them apart; it was everything. From the way they dressed—Mom in some shade of dark, whereas the darkest color I'd ever seen Aunt Julie wear was periwinkle—to their taste in food, Mom was on the spicy end of the spectrum and Aunt Julie was on the mild.

Mom stared at Aunt Julie.

Aunt Julie stared back at Mom.

This went on for twenty-one seconds. I counted. The last stare-down four years ago had gone forty-nine. So this was progress.

Finally, Aunt Julie folded her hands together, her rounded nails shining from a fresh manicure. "Hello, Jade. Hello, Megan."

Mom's back went ramrod straight when Aunt Julie referred to her by her given name. Aunt Julie was eight years older but acted more like her mother than her sister.

"How's it hangin', Jules?"

Aunt Julie's lips pursed hearing her little sister's nickname for her. Then she stepped back and motioned inside. "Well?"

That was my cue to pick up my luggage and follow after Mom, who was tromping up the front steps. "Are we done already? Really?" she asked, nudging Aunt Julie as she passed.

"I'm taking the higher road," Aunt Julie replied.

"What you call taking the higher road I call getting soft in your old age." Mom hustled through the door after that, like she was afraid Aunt Julie would kick her butt or something. The image of Aunt Julie kicking anything made me giggle to myself.

"Jade." Aunt Julie's smile was of the real variety this time as she took my duffel from me. "You were a girl the last time we saw you, and look at you now. All grown up."

"Hey, Aunt Julie. Thanks again for letting me spend the summer with you guys," I said, pausing beside her, not sure whether to hug her or keep moving. A moment of awkwardness passed before she made the decision for me by reaching out and patting my back. I continued on after that.

Aunt Julie wasn't cold or removed; she just showed her affection differently. But I knew she cared about me and my mom. If she didn't, she wouldn't pick up the phone on the first ring whenever we did call every few months. She also wouldn't have immediately said yes when Mom asked her a few months ago if I could spend the summer here.

"Let me show you to your room." She pulled the door shut behind her and led us through the living room. "Paul and I had the guest room redone to make it more fitting for a teenage girl."

"Instead of an eighty-year-old nun who had a thing for quilts and angel figurines?" Mom said, biting at her chipped black nail polish.

"I wouldn't expect someone whose idea of a feng shui living space is kicking the dirty clothes under their bed to appreciate my sense of style," Aunt Julie fired back, like she'd been anticipating Mom's dig.

I cut in before they could get into it. "You didn't have to do that, Aunt Julie. The guest room exactly the way it was would have been great."

"Speaking of the saint also known as my brother-in-law, where is Paul?" Mom spun around, moving down the hall backward.

"At work." Aunt Julie stopped outside a room. "He wanted to be here, but his job's been crazy lately."

Aunt Julie snatched the porcelain angel Mom had picked

up from the hall table. She carefully returned it to the exact same spot, adjusting it a hair after a moment's consideration.

"Where are the twins?" I asked, scanning the hallway for Hannah and Hailey. The last time I'd seen them, they were in preschool but acted like they were in grad school or something. They were nice kids, just kind of freakishly well behaved and brainy.

"At Chinese camp," Aunt Julie answered.

"Getting to eat dim sum and make paper dragons?" Mom asked, sounding almost surprised.

Aunt Julie sighed. "Learning the Chinese *language*." Aunt Julie opened a door and motioned me inside. I'd barely set one foot into the room before my eyes almost crossed from what I found.

Holy pink.

Hot pink, light pink, glittery pink, Pepto-Bismol pink— every shade, texture, and variety of pink seemed to be represented inside this square of space.

"What do you think?" Aunt Julie gushed, moving up beside me with a giant smile.

"I love it," I said, working up a smile. "It's great. So great. And so . . . pink."

"I know, right?" Aunt Julie practically squealed. I didn't know she was capable of anything close to that high-pitched. "We hired a designer and everything. I told her you were a girly seventeen-year-old and let her do the rest."

Glancing over at the full-length mirror framed in, you bet, fuchsia rhinestones, I wondered what about me led my aunt to classify me as "girly." I shopped at vintage thrift stores, lived in faded denim and colors found in nature, not ones manufactured in the land of Oz. I was wearing sneakers, cut-offs, and a flowy olive-colored blouse, pretty much the other end of the spectrum. The last girly thing I'd done was wear makeup on Halloween. I was a zombie.

Beside me, Mom was gaping at the room like she'd walked in on a crime scene. A gruesome crime scene.

"What the . . . *pink*?" she edited after I dug an elbow into her.

"You shouldn't have." I smiled at Aunt Julie when she turned toward me, still beaming.

"Yeah, Jules. You *really* shouldn't have." Mom shook her head, flinching when she noticed the furry pink stool tucked beneath the vanity that was resting beneath a huge cotton-candy-pink chandelier.

"It's the first real bedroom this girl's ever had. Of course I should have. I couldn't not." Aunt Julie moved toward the bed, fixing the smallest fold in the comforter.

"Jade's had plenty of bedrooms." Mom nudged me, glancing at the window. She was giving me an out. She had no idea how much more it would take than a horrendously pink room for me to want to take it.

"Oh, please. Harry Potter had a more suitable bedroom in that closet under the stairs than Jade's ever had. You can't consider something that either rolls down a highway or is bolted to a hotel floor an appropriate room for a young woman." Aunt Julie wasn't in dig mode; she was in honest mode.

That put Mom in unleash-the-beast mode.

Her face flashed red, but before she could spew whatever comeback she had stewing inside, I cut in front of her. "Aunt

Julie, would you mind if Mom and I had a few minutes alone? You know, to say good-bye and everything?"

As infrequently as we visited the house on Providence Avenue, I fell into my role of referee like it was second nature.

"Of course not. We'll have lots of time to catch up." Aunt Julie gave me another pat on the shoulder as she headed for the door. "We'll have all summer." She'd just disappeared when her head popped back in the doorway. "Meg, can I get you anything to drink before you have to dash?"

"Whiskey," Mom answered intently.

Aunt Julie chuckled like she'd made a joke, continuing down the hall.

I dropped my duffel on the pink zebra-striped throw rug. "Mom—"

"You grew up seeing the world. Experiencing things most people will never get to in their whole lives." Her voice was getting louder with every word. "You've got a million times the perspective of kids your age. A billion times more compassion and an understanding that the world doesn't revolve around you. Who is she to make me out to be some inadequate parent when all she cares about is raising obedient, genius robots? She doesn't know what it was like for me. How hard it was."

"Mom," I repeated, dropping my hands onto her shoulders as I looked her in the eye. "You did great."

It took a minute for the red to fade from her face, then another for her posture to relax. "*You're* great. I just tried not to get in the way too much and screw all that greatness up."

"And if you must know, I'd take any of the hundreds of rooms we've shared over this pinktastrophe." So it was kind of a lie, the littlest of ones. Sure, pink was on my offensive list, but the room was clean and had a door, and I would get to stay in the same place at least for the next few months. After living out of suitcases and overnight bags for most of my life, I was looking forward to discovering what drawer-and-closet living was like.

Mom threw her arms around me, pulling me in for one of those final-feeling hugs. Except this time, it kind of *was* a final one. Realizing that made me feel like someone had stuffed a tennis ball down my throat.

"I love you no matter what," she whispered into my ear again, the same words she'd sang, said, or on occasion shouted at me. Mom never just said *I love you*. She had something against those three words on their own. They were too open, too loosely defined, too easy to take back when something went wrong.

I love you no matter what had always been her way of telling me she loved me forever and for always. Unconditionally. She said that, before me, she'd never felt that type of love for anyone. What I'd picked up along the way on my own was that I was the only one she felt loved her back in the same way.

Squeezing my arms around my mom a little harder, I returned her final kind of hug. "I love you no matter what, too."

Chapter Two

I was still staring through the bedroom window at the spot where Mom's taxi had disappeared. I wondered if she was looking out of her window, too.

My lip took the brunt of my nervous energy as my mind ran through a million worst-case scenarios when I thought about Mom on her own.

I tried reassuring myself that she'd be okay. She had those fancy agents and support staff that came with hitting it big. And she had her bandmates . . . which didn't give me much confidence, since I was the most adult of all of them. Probably put together. But they took care of one another.

She'd be okay. Everything would be fine.

I wasn't sure how long I'd been at that window when a soft knock sounded at the bedroom door.

"Come on in!" I forced myself from my perch and pasted on an unaffected face.

"I wanted to see if you'd like any help unpacking," Aunt Julie started as she stepped into the room. Her eyes landed on my suitcase and duffel, in the same spot they'd been dumped, still zippered closed. "Or some help getting *started* unpacking."

I was so used to living out of suitcases, I hadn't gotten around to thinking about putting away my stuff yet. There were so many other things that needed to be experienced before settling in, but Aunt Julie was on a mission. She was rolling up the sleeves of her crisp white oxford and tucking her hair behind her ears.

"Sounds like a plan," I said, grabbing my duffel, since Aunt Julie had already had dibs on the suitcase.

"We're so happy you're here, Jade. I know we haven't seen each other a lot and we only talk every once in a while, but you're family and you're welcome here anytime. I hope you know that."

Tossing my duffel onto the bed, I tugged open the zipper. "I know that."

"Truthfully, I'm surprised you never asked to stay before when we offered." Aunt Julie's forehead creased after she threw the suitcase top open. "A summer on the California coast is most teenagers' dream."

Shrugging, I dislodged my array of sunscreens and lined them up on the dresser in descending SPF order. "I love being on the road with Mom. Seeing new things. Meeting new people. Each day different from the last."

Aunt Julie unfolded my favorite pair of jeans in front of her, her eyes widening when she saw the holes in the knees and how "loved" they were. I'd found them at some vintage store up in Portland a few months ago and wore them all the time. Whoever owned them before me had worn them all the time, too, so they'd seen a lot of mileage.

"What made you decide to take us up on our offer this summer, then? This is the first time your mom's band is headlining, so it seems like you really wouldn't want to miss it." She folded the jeans back up neatly and tucked them into the bottom drawer of the dresser. As far back as they could be shoved.

"It's also my last summer before I'll graduate and be heading off to college." I grabbed my shower bag next, realizing I'd actually have a reason to unpack it and spread things on a counter. "I wanted to see what this suburban, normal-ish lifestyle is all about."

Aunt Julie laughed. "I bet you'll find you enjoy having a routine, a schedule, a stable environment. What your mother was thinking hauling a young girl around the world chasing some silly dream is beyond me."

She said it in a nice enough tone, but her words hit me wrong. Almost like she was questioning my mom's parenting.

"I had a routine. It *was* a stable environment."

"Jade, honey, the longest you ever stayed anywhere was two weeks."

My shoulders lifted as I rummaged around in my duffel. "The scenery might have changed, but not much else did. Mom was always there for me, the other band members, too. I had school, hung out with friends, had my hobbies. Our location on the map might have been different, but nothing else was."

Aunt Julie continued to unfold every item in my suitcase, trying to disguise the surprised look in her eyes when she unearthed yet another thrift store gem. "Friends? How did you manage to make any when your mom uprooted you every other hour?"

"I learned to be really friendly." I shot a big cheesy grin at her that made her smile, too.

"And homeschooling? Your mom didn't even graduate high school. How can she expect to teach her daughter things she never learned herself?" When Aunt Julie came to her third pair of cutoffs, in the same condition as the other two, she gave up unpacking with a sigh. There wasn't anything pink and pristine in there, if that was what she was hoping to find.

"Mom got her GED." I could tell she wanted to say something to that, but she didn't. "And she spends hours studying my lesson plans to make sure she's got it before it comes my way."

Aunt Julie's eyebrows disappeared into her hairline. "Meg flunked geometry. And biology, if I remember correctly."

And chemistry and home economics, too. "Some of the harder stuff we go over together. We've got a system. It works."

Aunt Julie sighed again as I searched for topics to steer the conversation away from my mom. Aunt Julie might have loved her sister, but she couldn't talk about her without sounding like my mom had betrayed her in a hundred different ways, a thousand separate times.

"You obviously want to go to college. It's irresponsible of your mother to not have done a better job to set you up for success." She paused, biting something back. "I'll find you a tutor for the summer. Someone good. Excellent. Someone who can try to catch you up with your peers."

"Actually, Aunt Julie," I cut in. "I've been ahead of my peers since kindergarten. No need to go in search of that good-excellent tutor. But thanks."

"Just because your mom says you're gifted doesn't mean

a top university will, sweetie. Sorry if that sounds harsh, but it's the truth."

My gaze wandered to the window again. I seriously needed a fresh-air break before I said something I'd regret. "No, but those tests I take at the end of every school year do. Oh, and those SAT score things, too." I shot her a pleasant smile, watching her reaction. From doubt to surprise, and a couple more repeats, all in less than ten seconds.

Before she could say anything else, I grabbed my cloth purse from the bed and threw it over my shoulder. "Do you mind if I go out and explore for a while? You know, get my bearings in this new land of suburbia?" I felt kind of weird asking for permission. Usually with Mom, I simply told her where I was heading and when I'd be back, but I guessed Aunt Julie wouldn't be so chill.

From the look on her face you would have thought I'd asked to streak down the block a few laps. "Where do you have in mind? We could head to the mall together and buy you some new clothes?"

The m-word. I shuddered at the idea. I hadn't set foot in one since I was four and Mom tried dragging me kicking and screaming to visit some lame Santa in Sarasota. We hadn't made it past the double doors at the entrance before she turned around and let go of her plan to torture me with spilling my guts to some stinky mall Santa.

"Actually, I was thinking I'd wander around on my own two feet. See what there is to see."

"You don't have anywhere particular in mind?"

Uh-oh. The tone. The one that was created to make teenagers feel like they didn't have a clue. Time to improvise before I got to experience the summer in a proverbial cell, or worse.

"I was thinking about finding a summer job. That's what a lot of teenagers do, right?"

Aunt Julie started to relax. A little. "Well, yeah, sure. I suppose so. Where did you have in mind?"

Anywhere besides the mall?

While I thought of a way to voice this without sounding like I was insulting her apparent love affair with my personal nightmare in brick-and-mortar form, she snapped her fingers. "You know, when I drove by the public pool earlier, I saw a sign saying they were still hiring for the summer. Is that something that might interest you?"

I think I visibly sagged with relief. "Yes!" I practically shouted. "That sounds perfect."

As Aunt Julie gave me directions, I tried not to look overly eager because I guessed that would alert her. I knew living together would come with plenty of growing pains. I might have been one of the more responsible teenagers around, but I'd lived on more parental trust than most of my peers.

Since I suspected Aunt Julie and Uncle Paul wouldn't be so laid-back about letting me come and go, I wanted to ease them into the idea. They had to see I could be trusted, so that when I asked to head out for a few hours, their minds didn't automatically picture me as the main attraction at some drunken orgy.

"Do you want me to drive you?" Aunt Julie asked, already reaching for her purse as we made it down the hall.

"It was a long flight and it's such a nice day, I'd like to walk. If you don't mind," I tacked on for good measure. If

I'd said that to my mom, she would have stared at me like I'd grown a second head.

"It's a bit of a walk. Little more than a mile. You should probably take Uncle Paul's bike, just in case."

I decided not to bring up that I frequently walked several miles to find a gas station that served Icees. At this point, I'd unicycle my way there if it meant getting a little alone time.

"The bike sounds great."

Chapter Three

So the bike wasn't great. Like at all.

And I'd ridden my share of bikes in various stages of disrepair. From the amount of dust that was caked on the seat, I'd guess the last time Uncle Paul had ridden it was in a former life. The chain squeaked so loudly people were turning their heads two blocks down when they heard me coming—or at least it squeaked when it wasn't falling off the gears. The brakes worked, though. It might have sounded like I was bringing a freight train to a stop whenever I tapped them, but they did their job.

By the time I finally coaxed this so-called efficient means of transportation to the public pool Aunt Julie had told me about, I could have walked there and back again twice. Walking also would have been the preferred option, as I was now showing up to ask about a job with grease-painted hands and arms. Plus, with all the baking I'd done on the sidewalk servicing the lemon of a bike, I was sweaty and hot and, yep, I had pit stains I observed as I leaned the "bike" up against the chain-link fence surrounding the pool. There was a bike rack, and Aunt Julie had given me a lock, but no one was going to steal this thing. I wasn't that lucky.

Inside, kids were screaming and splashing while parents saw to their tans and newsfeeds. It didn't seem like too bad a place to work for a summer. I could be outside, which was always a plus—with my SPF in place and reapplied every 90 to 120 minutes—it was close by, and people came here to have fun.

As summer jobs went, this one was golden. Hopefully they still needed someone, as the huge nylon sign strung from the fence facing the busy road suggested.

When I approached the gate, I didn't see anyone sitting inside the office to check people in or hand out job applications. Maybe there'd be a stack of them sitting out, so I could grab one and return it when I didn't look like I'd recently fought an entire legion of grease monsters.

I wasn't that lucky—*again*. Should have known.

After waiting a few minutes, I considered tracking down a lifeguard to see if they knew how to hunt down an application. As I started to move toward the pool, my phone chimed. I'd already missed three texts from Aunt Julie.

Did you make it there okay?

Jade, are you at the pool?

And finally the last one: I bet you're turned around. Where are you? I'm on my way.

Punching in a quick text to let her know I was okay and yes, I was here at the pool, I exhaled when she got right back to me.

Phew. Let me know when you leave so I know when to expect you.

Holy helicopter parenting. Mom could have paid a little more attention, maybe, but Aunt Julie's style was off-the-charts suffocating.

A middle-aged woman finally burst into the office, appearing flustered and exhausted all at once. "I'm sorry. Have you been waiting here awhile?" She hustled up to the counter like getting me taken care of was a matter of life and death.

"Only a minute or two," I said, wiping my hands on my cutoffs to try to get some of the grease off. It wasn't that easy, though.

"One for admission?" She wiped her sweaty forehead off with a paper towel, breathing like she'd finished a four-minute mile.

"Actually, I'm checking to see if you're still hiring." I clasped my hands behind my back when I saw the rubbing had only made the streaks worse.

The woman practically collapsed into the chair behind her. "You have no idea exactly how much we're hiring." Yanking open a metal drawer, she riffled through some papers before pulling a packet free. "Can you pass a background check?"

Oh, crap. Was this, like, *the* person who was hiring? The manager? I stopped wiping at the grease on my shorts and turned my attention to panicking about my sizable pit stains.

A quick check at her nametag, where the words POOL MANAGER were stamped below JANET, confirmed my suspicion.

On the bright side, she wasn't exactly looking fresh as a daisy herself.

"Well, hon? Background check?" Janet asked, waving an

application at me. "There's no sense wasting your time filling one of these out if it's not going to come back clean."

"That depends which states you run one in," I dead-panned. When I realized what I'd said and how Janet had taken it, I raised my greasy hands. "Sorry, that was a joke. A *bad* joke," I added as I watched the crease between Janet's eyebrows carve a canyon. "Yes, I can clear a background check. I've never committed any crimes. In any states. Or foreign countries—or territories, for that matter."

Great, I'd officially botched my first attempt at getting a job.

"When could you start?" Janet scooted the application across the counter toward me.

"Right away."

She blinked at me, like she was gauging my level of seri-ousness. "What's your schedule like?"

"Wide open," I answered with a shrug.

"Good. You're hired."

If it had been physically possible, my jaw would have hit the ground. "For real?"

"On the condition that your background check really does come back clean and you really can start right away. Good-ness knows we need you." Glancing back at the pool deck, Janet waved over at one of the lifeguards.

"Thank you for the job, that's great," I stammered, "But, uh, can I ask what that job is?"

I was holding my breath that she wasn't going to say life-guard, because I didn't have the heart to tell her I wasn't certified for that, but instead, she pointed at a stand sitting in the back corner of the pool deck. There was a big window

23

propped open with what looked to be a soda machine and a display of chips and candy out front, but no one was actually inside to help the growing line of people waiting.

"A concession employee. Scooping ice cream, making hot dogs, that kind of thing." Janet set the application papers in front of me and handed me a pen, like she wasn't going to let me leave until I'd filled it out.

"What's the schedule like?" I asked, taking the pen and starting to fill in the first part of the application.

"Are you eighteen yet?"

I shook my head. "Seventeen."

Janet muttered something else under her breath. "Then it will be four to five days a week." She didn't ask if that would work. I don't think she cared, as long as I kept filling out the paperwork.

"When do you want me to start?" I moved on to the next section.

"Tomorrow."

She said it so quickly, I glanced up to see if she was being serious. She was. "Will all the paperwork be done and cleared by then?"

"For my situation here at present, it sure will be." Janet winced when a family the size of a small village jumped into the back of the concession stand line. "I've got to get back there, but leave everything right here when you're done, and I'll see you tomorrow at ten."

"Really? That's it?" I'd never have guessed getting a first job would be so easy.

"I usually like all of our new employees to sit down and meet with the head lifeguard, too, but he's on a break and

I've got a crowd of people about to tip that stand if I don't get out there. You can meet him tomorrow." Janet started jogging away when she stopped herself. "Oh, the pay starts at twelve-fifty, but"—she said the *but* so fast it was like she was waiting for me to complain or back out—"there are opportunities for a raise after putting in a couple of weeks, and then again a month after that. So at the end of the summer, you could be earning almost as much as the starting lifeguards."

I smiled like this was fantastic news. The truth was I'd never been a big spender. Plus, I wanted the job to give me something to do and to get me out of the house.

"Sounds great. Thanks again!" I lifted my pen, feeling lame for thanking my boss for a job the way a person thanked a barista for their coffee, then finished the application as quickly as I could.

After double-checking to make sure I'd filled in all the boxes and signed all the signature lines, I dropped the papers onto the desk and headed back to Lemon. I'd probably wind up having to carry the thing back home, instead of the other way around.

Right before I got to the bike, I noticed someone behind the steering wheel of the old truck I was passing. He was about my age and had a dark pair of sunglasses hiding his eyes. At first I thought he was staring at me as I struggled to yank Lemon away from the fence—both the pedal and handlebar kept getting hung up in the chain-link.

It wasn't until I'd ripped the bike free and fallen back a few steps, giving me a better view through the rolled-down window, that I realized he wasn't staring—he was sleeping. Like the kind of sleep that people call comatose.

It was baking hot out here on the sidewalk in the sun; I couldn't imagine how much hotter it was inside the cab of a truck. I could see beads of sweat dotting his face and neck, and even though his mouth was parted from what I guessed was deep breathing, I couldn't see his chest moving.

Moving closer, the bike protesting in squeaks and creaks, I leaned in the window. I was really infringing on this guy's personal space, but I did not want to be one of those people who ignored someone who might need help.

He wasn't wearing a shirt. Which made it easier to confirm that he was still breathing since, yeah . . . chest.

I reassured myself as I crept another step closer, my eyes locked on a part of his body that had at least a little to do with respiration. I was just a Good Samaritan making sure this stranger I was not at all remotely attracted to wasn't experiencing heatstroke or a heart attack, I told myself as I took in his skin, sheeny with sweat and golden from the sun.

Speaking of hearts, mine was misbehaving.

Back up, Jade. Slow your roll. It's just a boy. One of those creatures you've run across only a few million times in your life. It's not like he's the last boy on the planet or even the cutest one you've ever come across.

Maybe.

Back. Up. Jade.

Right as I was leaning out of his truck, something inside blasted with noise. I jumped so hard, I smacked the back of my head against the door frame.

"Ouch," I yelped, rubbing at the spot I'd whacked.

The guy inside went from the sleeping dead to alert and awake like a switch had been flipped.

The boy grabbed something on the seat and rammed it to his ear. "Hello?" he half-hollered, his sunglasses falling off from all the jolting around. "Hello?" he repeated, louder and slightly more frantic this time.

Okay, so he was awake, but not so alert.

"It's your alarm," I said, still massaging my head. That was going to leave a mark.

His phone was still propped to his ear and blaring, and his forehead creased as he turned his head. From the look on his face, he clearly wasn't expecting to find someone hovering right outside his parked truck. Where he'd just been sleeping. Shirtless. And perfect.

Don't make me threaten to lobotomize whatever boy-crazed part of your brain seemed to sprout from nowhere, Jade Abbott.

"Huh?" he said, blinking awake, still staring at me like he couldn't figure out what the hell I was doing here.

"Your phone. It's an alarm going off, not a call." I pointed at the screen. "I have the same chime on mine."

His head tipped. "Huh?"

Okay, so he was nice to look at, but there wasn't much else going on past that ever so attractive exterior.

"Just . . . here." Reaching inside the cab, I swiped my finger across the screen to turn the alarm off. The phone stopped screaming at us. I could feel the boy looking at me, like he was waiting for me to say something. "So, uh, have a nice day," I said, starting to walk away, Lemon screeching beside me.

"Have a nice day?" he repeated after me, sounding almost as dumbfounded as I felt.

I smiled weakly and kept going. Maybe he'd let it go.

That's when I heard the sound of a door swinging open. "Hey, hold up," he called. "You can't just gawk and bounce like that."

I skidded to a stop. "I wasn't gawking at you. I was checking on you."

He huffed. "Yeah, you were checking, all right. Checking me out."

A rush of anger flashed through me. I most certainly had been checking on him. At least at first.

Spinning around, I had to yank Lemon along with me. "I think you need to cross-check your definition of checking out. Because there's a big difference between making sure a person's still breathing and that person making you pant."

A slow smile spread as he closed the truck door behind him. He was taller than he'd appeared stuffed inside the cab, and the rest of him followed the chest theme—built, golden, and nice to look at. Too bad that was the only nice part about him.

"Is that why you're breathing so hard right now?" he said. "Because I make you pant?"

Flames licked up my throat until I felt like I could breathe fire if I opened my mouth. That was partly what I was hoping would come out. Instead, I said, "Yes, of course *you're* the reason why I'm breathing so hard right now. Not because it's ungodly hot and I thought I'd come across a dead person only to have that not-dead person wake up and start accusing me of being some Peeping Tom."

"I'm not accusing you of being a Peeping Tom. I don't even know your name. Once you give it to me, then I can accuse you properly of being a Peeping Whoever."

My eyes narrowed as I contemplated hopping on Lemon and taking off, only to remember this hunk of junk could barely take me a total of two feet before busting its chain or insert-some-other-bike-part-here. I didn't need to give this guy any other reason to make fun of me.

"So, what's that name?" He curled his hand around the wall of his truck bed, bracing himself.

"Up. Yours."

He nodded, fighting a smile. "Unusual name. Exotic-sounding. French?"

"I've got a few French words I can give you." *Tête-merde, va te faire enculer,* and *imbecile* all popped to mind.

"Always been a fan of the French. Gave the world some of my favorite things." His expression filled in the rest.

I should have had a comeback for that. I should have had a dozen. I was fast on my feet and not easily rattled. Perks of being raised with a wiseass of a mother. But nothing came. Nada. I wasn't sure if it was the heat or feeling out of my element or this boy, but I felt off my game. Way off. The only way to get the last word in was to turn my back and walk away. So Lemon and I turned to make our noisy exit.

"Hey, Up Yours?" Hot Obnoxious Boy called after me as I rolled Lemon away. "Next time you can just leave the tip on my dash. The first gawk's complimentary, but the ones after are going to cost you."

Powering on, I glared at the sidewalk. The first "gawk" had cost me plenty already, my dignity topping that list. I wasn't giving him one more thing.

Chapter Four

By dinnertime, I'd already forgotten all about what happened earlier that day. I couldn't even remember what *he* looked like or much about *him* at all.

At least that was the story I tried to sell myself. Too bad myself wasn't in the market for falsehoods and fabrications.

"I can't believe the pool's having you start tomorrow. Don't you want to have some time to unwind and relax?" Aunt Julie was drying the pots I was washing. She'd offered to do it, but I'd said I wanted to. It felt good scrubbing the heck out of some hard surface. Not that I had any pent-up frustration or anything from what may or may not have happened earlier.

"They need someone right away. I think the manager would have started me today if she could have," I answered, handing Aunt Julie the last dish in the sink.

"Well, they're lucky to have you. But if it becomes too much, don't be afraid to say something. Working five days a week is a lot for someone your age."

If Aunt Julie thought twentyish hours a week was a lot

to work for someone my age, she should have seen what I juggled on the road with Mom. Between schoolwork, homework, setup, teardown, and all-around everyday life management, I probably worked two full-time jobs. But I liked it. I liked staying busy and doing stuff. I wasn't one of those people content to lounge on a couch and watch reruns of whatever reality television show was the latest and greatest train wreck of the hour.

"I'm sorry about the bike. If I'd known it was in such a state of disrepair, I would have insisted on driving you." Aunt Julie looked over at me with an anxious gleam in her eyes, like she was under the impression I was made of porcelain and capable of shattering from the slightest of mishaps.

"Oh, it wasn't too bad. I think I got it all fixed up," I downplayed as I pulled the drain plug. I wouldn't have mentioned anything about the bike, but Aunt Julie had been stationed at the big window when I came back, practically cradling the beast in my arms after the front tire had gone flat. You know, after the chain had fallen off three more times on the return trip, and the right pedal decided to fly off.

"I never knew you were so handy fixing things up," said Aunt Julie.

"I learned it on tour. There was always something breaking down or needing to be fixed. Whether it was a bus, a speaker, or a bike. Mom told me I should open a fix-it shop. She said we could call it Jade's Junkyard." Saying her name made my stomach twist with a pinch of homesickness. At least I think that's what it was. I'd never felt it before, because I'd never been away from my mom for longer than a few hours, when she was performing onstage.

"Jade's Junkyard? I don't know if that would be such a promising—"

"Mom wasn't serious about that, Aunt Julie. It was just something she'd say."

"Oh. Good." When she sighed with relief, it was like I'd told her I turned down pledging to the biker gang I was invited into.

After spending the past couple of hours hanging with Aunt Julie—the twins had a sleepover at Chinese camp—I was starting to wonder if she and my mom had any similarities at all. I had yet to find one. I mean, other than both being female and born with the same last name.

"I stopped by one of the specialty bakeries in town and picked up a couple of vegan brownies. In the mood for some dessert?" Aunt Julie shot me a smile as she covered Uncle Paul's dinner plate with plastic wrap. It was almost eight o'clock and he still wasn't back from work. It was no wonder Aunt Julie had plopped into a lawn chair beside me in the garage earlier when I was tinkering on the bike.

"Vegan brownies? Really?" I dried my hands, eyeing the tray of chocolate goodness. "You didn't have to do that, Aunt Julie. I told you I'm good figuring out my own meals. I don't want you to have to kill yourself trying to feed me."

She tsked as she carefully placed Uncle Paul's dinner in the fridge. "Oh, please. It would do us all good to eat more veggies and fruit anyway. I've already picked up a few recipe books and stocked the cupboards."

I leaned into the counter as I watched my aunt motion into the packed fridge before moving on to open the pantry. She really had stocked up on food that I could eat.

"Wow. That's amazing. I think I'll be set for the rest of the summer." I smiled, especially when I saw the amount of tofu she'd loaded up on. The whole top shelf in the fridge was stuffed with it.

She inspected her haul with me, then gave a nod of approval before closing everything up again. "I'm sorry Paul couldn't be here for your first night. I know he wanted to be."

"Don't even worry about it. He's a busy guy." I shrugged it off, knowing Uncle Paul was some kind of big-shot business-man who did something in finance. From the sound of it, his latest promotion kept him away more nights than he was home. "What's the girls' schedule going to look like for the summer?" Even though they were about as different from me as Aunt Julie was from Mom, they were the only cousins I had. Or at least the only ones I knew of. I wanted to get to know them and spend at least some time with them.

She freed a couple of small china plates from the cup-board. "I enrolled them in several camps for the summer. Chinese this week, then there's violin camp, a STEM-based camp, and ballet camp at the end of summer."

"Wow. That's a lot of camp."

Aunt Julie nodded at me, her face glowing. "So you and I will have lots of time to spend together."

I painted on a smile and thanked her as she slid a per-fectly centered brownie across the counter at me, a gleaming fork propped across the plate.

This was the fanciest brownie I'd ever eaten. Usually Mom and I just dug them out of the pan with our fingers.

"Do you mind if I take my dessert to go?" I asked. "I still need to finish unpacking, and then I'm going to crash. I'm pooped." From the flight to the malfunctioning bike to the disaster with Hot and Obnoxious, it had been a full day.

"Do you want some help?" Aunt Julie was already grabbing her brownie plate and coming around the counter.

"No." It came out a little too loud, so I reined it in. "No, thank you. You've already done so much. I think I'm going to try calling Mom to see if I can catch her during a layover or something." Picking up my plate, I left the kitchen. "Thanks for everything, Aunt Julie. You've been awesome."

She gave me a funny look, like she wasn't familiar with the phrase. Then her eyes softened and her smile moved into place. "You're pretty *awesome* yourself, kid," she said, picking up her fork as she leaned into the counter. It was the most relaxed I'd ever seen my aunt. "If you need anything, you know where to find me."

Waving goodnight, I ambled up the stairs and down the hall, trying to remember which door belonged to my bedroom for the summer. Their house wasn't overly huge to the point of being offensive, but it was pretty big. Especially to someone who'd spent her life dwelling in tour buses and motel rooms.

I picked the right door, the third one on the left, and braced myself for the explosion of pink that hit me as soon as I stepped inside. *Pink.* It was the dirtiest four-letter word I knew. Next to *mall*.

Reminding myself of how well-intentioned Aunt Julie had been to put this together for me, I closed the door behind me and headed for my bags. We'd put away most everything, but I wanted to take time to find exactly the right spot for my journals and books. Because Mom and I were always moving, I'd never been able to have the serious collection of books I'd always wanted, so I made good use of those mini libraries that had been cropping up all over the country. However, I had personal copies of a handful of my all-time Austen and Brontë favorites. I didn't care about how much extra weight they added to my ever-moving suitcase—it was poundage well worth it. I'd rather live with one pair of Toms and get rid of the rest of my shoes than have to part with my books.

The journals didn't take up as much room. They weren't really journals, but pretty books filled with blank pages I used to scribble down whatever story or thought was working around in my head. I'd written short stories, poems, even a novella or two. I scratched down words that caught my attention, random phrases and meaningful quotes. I loved to write.

At first, Mom thought that love of writing had come from her love of writing music, but I told a different kind of story with my words. Her stories she shared with millions; my stories I kept to myself.

Spinning a few circles around the bedroom, I decided the window seat facing the front yard was the ideal spot to store my precious belongings. A heap of blankets and pillows had been spread around on it—forget about the color—and it seemed like the perfect place to spend a few minutes or a few hours lost in someone else's words or my own.

After tucking my journals and books on the window ledge and rearranging them a few times until they were in precisely the right order, I shimmied out of my cutoffs and flopped down.

I could have fallen asleep right then if I'd closed my eyes, but I hadn't gone to bed without reading or writing in forever. It was my bedtime ritual.

Since I was more tired than normal tonight, I went with the reading option.

I'd just finished *Wuthering Heights* on the flight here, so I debated which one to start next. Or, more accurately, which one to reread next for the one thousandth time. My fingers made the decision before my mind did.

No sooner had I opened up to the first worn page of *Jane Eyre* when an envelope came spilling out. I recognized the handwriting right away. As I opened it, I checked my phone to see if Mom had texted me back after I sent her one earlier. Still nothing.

I was so used to my mom getting back to me a second after I needed her, but I knew I'd have to adjust to this thousands-of-miles-of-separation thing. She wasn't the only one who'd have to adapt to me going away to college in a year.

A shiny plastic card fell from the letter when I opened it. A credit card. With my name on it and everything.

Tucking the card into the middle of the book, I read the letter.

The card's for emergencies. Not for you to max out at the mall. That was followed by a funny face with its tongue sticking out, because Mom was as avid a mall hater as I was. *This summer, I want you to put down those books and journals and go live your life. I want them to collect dust, you're so busy living. You've always put others first, and I adore you for that, but for once I want you to put you first. Do something you never dreamed you would. Befriend someone wholly unlike you. Go so far out of your comfort zone you start to squirm. Because, Jade, the only things we're going to one day regret are the things we never did. Do everything. Do anything. Just do. It's a verb, baby, which means action. I promise the books will be waiting for you at the end of summer. I love you no matter what. Even if you really do max this card out at the mall. Kick Summer's Ass. Love, Mom.*

I started crying pretty much right from the start. The kind of sobbing that rocked your body and made you gasp in tiny, shallow breaths. Maybe it was because I missed Mom like crazy and it hadn't even been twenty-four hours since we'd said good-bye. Maybe it was because of what happened earlier at the pool, compounded by the other stresses of the day. Or maybe I was crying because I needed a good cry.

My whole life I'd dreamed of experiencing a summer just like this one, and now that I was, the responsibility of making it count felt crippling. I was holding my wish in the palm of my hand, and suddenly I felt terrified I was going to ruin it.

Chapter Five

I was always an early riser, one of the few in my age group. I liked sunrises and how quiet and still everything was. Like anything was possible. I was a night owl, though, too. Sunsets came with their own stillness. The result of being both a morning and a night person meant I lived in a constant state of sleep deprivation, but it didn't bother me.

So by the time I was departing on the new and improved Lemon a little before nine-thirty a.m. the next day, I'd already had a full morning: an early walk, a little more reading, some writing, breakfast, and a solid hour of online reconnaissance.

No, I wasn't training to become a spy or considering a bounty-hunting career. I was scouring the Internet for something far more dangerous—my biological father.

Not that he was a dangerous person, at least that I knew of, but it was a hazardous topic where Mom was concerned. She didn't know I'd spent half of the past year cyberstalking him. Or that he was a big reason I'd suggested spending the summer here in California. And she definitely didn't know

I was planning to come face to face with him before the summer ended.

If she did, there was no way she'd have let me stay. My mom and dad weren't on speaking terms. For the past eighteen years almost, or whatever the day was when she'd approached him to let him know she was pregnant with his child. I guess that was all it took for him to turn and run. From what I'd gathered over the past few months, he'd never stopped running.

Like Mom, he was in a band. Lead singer and guitarist, like her as well. His band didn't have the same kind of following or radio time as Mom's, but that might have had to do with him joining or starting a new band every few years. Kind of hard to build up a hard-core following when you kept changing your band's name and the style of music you rocked.

Robbie Devine, that was my dad's name. Unfortunately, not just his stage name. His real one. It was like he'd been born for rock 'n' roll. Mom hadn't said one thing to me about him willingly, but she always answered my questions when they came up.

When I started asking her for details about what happened, she just kind of shut down. She wasn't the one who informed me he'd run away when she told him she was pregnant; she gave me the softer version of it being a case of young love not panning out, the way most didn't. Aunt Julie told me the truth. We'd never had contact with him, and I knew that if it was up to Mom, we never would.

But how could I know who I was or who I wanted to be if I didn't know who I'd come from? Sure, I knew my mom as well as I knew myself, but I didn't know jack about the person who'd given me the other half of my DNA. I knew what he looked like now and basic facts, but I didn't know *him*. Until I did, I wasn't sure if I could really know who I was, either.

So that was the plan for the summer. One of them, at least. The big one. Operation Get to Know My Dad. Like with all monumental things in life, I was equal parts excited and terrified, but he was the guy who'd helped create me. He might have run, back when he was a scared seventeen-year-old, but that was almost two decades ago. A person could change.

His band would be playing at some venue in L.A. in August, so that gave me a little more time to put together a plan for how to walk up to some stranger, shake hands, and drop the *Hey, I'm your daughter* line on him.

I also needed to drop the bomb without Aunt Julie or Mom finding out, because she and my mom might have been on opposite sides of the court on everything else but the one thing these two seemed to agree on was my dad, both favoring the Harry Potter policy of not talking about He Who Must Not Be Named.

By the time I pedaled up to the pool, I was ready for my mind to be distracted by something other than my parents. Hopefully it would be as busy today as it had looked yesterday.

The pool wasn't open yet, but I could see a few employees moving around inside to get ready for the morning rush, so after settling Lemon into the bike rack, I made my way to the front gate.

"You showed up. Thank God." Janet heaved a relieved sigh when she saw me coming, already opening the gate for me.

"Did you think I wouldn't?" I asked.

"With the way my luck's been lately, no, not really. Plus, the concession positions are always the hardest to fill." She didn't say this until I'd walked in and she'd already locked the gate behind me.

"Why's that?" I asked, instantly wishing I'd brought my sunglasses. The glare on the pool deck was so bright I felt my corneas burning.

"Oh, you know." Janet flailed her hand as she powered toward the concession stand. I had to jog to keep up with her. "It's a busy job, and it doesn't come with all the fame and glory of the lifeguarding positions."

My shoulder lifted. "Yeah, but there's constant shade, a fan"—I motioned at the small fan attached to the lip of the counter when we stepped inside—"and I don't have to blow my whistle and yell at people to walk and not run. Sounds like a solid position to me."

Janet patted me on the back like I was the cutest little thing. "Do me a favor and hang on to that optimistic spark, kid." As she started to go through the stand door, she paused to pull an old yellowed binder from a drawer. "Here's the training manual. Feel free to go through this if you have a few minutes. Everything's in here." She tossed it onto the counter in front of me. It landed with a loud clomp. "Zoey will be in at twelve to help with the lunch rush, so she can answer your questions, too. Anything you need in the meanwhile is in the training binder." When Janet checked her watch, her eyes went Frisbee-wide. "If I were you, I'd spend the next nine minutes studying that first section before those gates open and the minivans start rolling up. You don't want to mistake the mustard for cheese sauce when you make a plate of nachos. Trust me."

"I will. Thanks," I said, already tearing open the binder, trying to separate the first and second pages, which seemed to be glued together by a sauce of questionable origin. "If I have any questions before Zoey gets in, who should I ask?"

Janet was already gone, powering across the pool deck. "The manual!" she hollered back. "Any questions, check the training manual."

Before I could panic, I reminded myself I was dishing up ice cream and making hot dogs. I'd managed all aspects of stage setup and teardown from the age of thirteen for the Shrinking Violets—this wasn't reinventing the wheel.

"Well, at least you can't laugh at me for asking a dumb question," I muttered to the training manual as I continued to work at the stuck-together pages. They came apart a moment later. Well, they *tore* apart a moment later.

On the upside, at least when it came time to patch the page back together, I could use the sauce of questionable substance (mustard, it turned out!) to fix it.

It felt like Janet had just left me alone when a herd of kids in bathing suits and goggles started charging into the pool. They slowed to a fast walk only after the lifeguards on duty blew a collective whistle to get them to stop running.

Haha. They were the whistle blowers. I was the one serving the kids ice cream. Who won at the end of the day?

Plus, I remembered, I had a fan. Except when I spun around to turn it on, I soon discovered it wasn't, in fact, a functioning fan.

As kids started to cannonball into the pool while moms claimed loungers, I tore through as many pages of the training manual as I could. Lucky for me I was a fast reader, because by the time my first customer padded up to the stand, I'd made it through a third of the material. I guessed the cleanup instructions could wait. The proper temperature for a hot dog to reach and how to handle the money could not.

I smiled down at my first customer, a cute little boy with hammerhead swim trunks and angelic blue eyes. This job was going to be a piece of cake.

"What can I get you, little man?"

His nostrils flared. Like literally flared. "I'm. Not. Little."

I leaned away from the counter. His voice made it clear I'd hit a sore spot.

"I didn't mean little as in short. Or small," I added, when the word *short* made his nostrils flare again. "I meant little as in young. That's all."

Now his eyes were narrowing. What was wrong with this kid?

"I'm. Not. Young."

I painted on a smile. It was met by the frown to rule all frowns. "What can I get you?" I repeated, making a mental note not to add any more commentary at the end of my questions. Or statements. Or anything. Not if I didn't want to be dropkicked by an army of *little* kids.

"Ice cream," he demanded, slamming down a twenty-dollar bill.

If this was one of the many kids I'd babysat while on tour with the Shrinking Violets, I would have waited until he remembered to tack on a please to that request, but I guessed my job had more to do with keeping the customers happy than teaching them manners.

"What flavor?"

The kid huffed, like that was a stupid question. "Chocolate."

Apparently that should have been obvious.

"Kid cone?" I guessed as I took the twenty and moved behind the till to ring up the order, realizing my mistake a second too late.

"No. Triple scoop." He practically barked at me.

No wonder the kid was such a turd. His blood sugar was all over the place, swimming in a vat of ice cream.

Ringing up the order, I took the money, gave him his change, and stacked three scoops of ice cream on a waffle cone as quickly as I could. Which wasn't quick at all, since the ice cream was as hard as a rock. At the end of the scooping session, my wrist felt like it was going to snap. Shark Boy took the cone and his change without so much as a look back.

I had one second to take a breather and roll my wrist a few times before I turned around to discover a line had formed stretching from the counter to almost the edge of the pool.

Swallowing, I scanned for help, but every other pool employee was putting out a fire of their own. The lifeguards were busy blowing whistles and waving their arms at kids doing something they weren't supposed to, and the front desk staff were tending to their own line at the front.

Giving myself an internal pep talk, I shielded my eyes—I was going to be blind by the end of the day—and leaned over the counter.

"What can I get you?" I kept the smile this time but ditched the add-on tag.

The girl, who was maybe a year or two older than the first boy, slapped down another twenty. "A triple-scoop cone."

This was going to be a long summer.

Chapter Six

My wrists weren't going to survive. I was going to have to check into voice dictation software to continue writing because the use of my hands was going to be over when my shift was.

Ice cream. And more ice cream. A couple of hot dogs and a few bags of chips. Ice cream. Ice cream. Ice. Cream.

I was convinced I could have filled the pool in front of me with the amount of ice cream I'd scooped to masses of bossy, manner-deficient *little* kids today.

Of course Zoey had called in saying she was running late, so I'd had to wing it on my own even longer than I expected. It wasn't even one and I already felt like I'd spent a fortnight stuffed in this hot tin can, baking in my supposed "shade." Sure, there was no direct sun hitting me, but it was easily fifteen degrees hotter in this thing, plus, out there on the pool deck, there was this nifty thing known as airflow. Something I'd left behind a few hours ago when I stepped into this inferno on wheels.

Sometime between when I was spooning my millionth

triple scoop of the day and handing it off before taking the next order, something appeared on the counter next to the till. Something I would have auctioned off a foot of my long hair for right then.

A pair of dark sunglasses; tucked beneath them was a piece of paper. On it, one word had been scribbled: *Sorry.*

That was all. Clearly it wasn't the ankle-biters standing in line. And what was my benefactor sorry for? That my eyes were permanently damaged, probably, and they hadn't dropped the glasses off sooner?

Whatever it was, I could think about later, because the hot dogs weren't going to make themselves. Slipping the sunglasses on, I could practically feel my corneas exhaling in relief.

It was amazing how much better my day became from that one small act of thoughtfulness. The heat felt less sweltering; the orders were less snotty-sounding; the ice cream felt almost softer to scoop.

Only, the line had gone from long to longer as the day progressed—it didn't seem to matter how fast I moved.

"What can I get you?" I asked the next kid in line.

The young girl lifted up onto her tiptoes and set a few dollars on the counter. "A hot dog with ketchup, please."

My shoulders sagged with relief as I rang her up, my faith in humanity restored.

"Coming right up," I half-sang as I started whipping together a hot dog, swirling on a pretty ribbon of ketchup.

That was when I noticed someone standing in line, one of the few "big" people I'd seen brave the never-ending stream of kids. But this one was extra-big. And shirtless.

Hold up. I recognized those abs.

Holy crap.

Thanks to the sunglasses, I pretended not to see him, and since he'd been gazing over at the pool, I knew he hadn't caught me looking. Yet. It wouldn't be long before he'd make it through the line to the counter and start giving me a hard time for ogling the heck out of him again because, you know, I had to make general eye contact to take his order.

And here I'd been convinced that yesterday was the first and last I'd ever see of that egomaniac. What had I even been thinking when I'd had the briefest inkling that he was hot? He wasn't even. Not a little bit.

That's what I kept telling myself as I tried not to cast sideways looks at him, hovering there in line, arms crossed over his chest, jaw extra pronounced thanks to the way his head was turned, his hair falling in all the right directions, catching the sunshine.

I handed the hot dog I'd gone a little ketchup-happy on to the little girl before taking the next order. He was only a few more back and still hadn't noticed me as he shuffled a couple steps closer, his swim shorts sliding a little lower— just low enough for me to catch a glimpse of a ridge of muscle I should not have been noticing given my feelings for the pompous Neanderthal. *Smug, arrogant, bigheaded,* I sang to myself, starting to hum my insane melody out loud.

Trouble. Trouble. Trouble.

As I finished the next order, I noticed something I probably should have registered the moment I saw him—he was wearing a whistle.

The next trio of words my mind rattled off wasn't so PG-rated.

However, I didn't miss that he was in navy-colored shorts—not that I was hyperfocused on his shorts or anything—while the other guards were in red shorts or suits. Maybe he worked at a different pool and was filling in for the day. Maybe he was one of those on-call types, if there even was a thing like that. There was no way he could actually work here. Irony wasn't that mean—I hoped.

That was when I noticed Janet bustling up to the stand, a clipboard in one hand, her phone in the other, looking every bit as flustered and red-faced as I did.

She broke to a stop beside Trouble. "I just had to take Zach off the rotation and lay him down in the office. Heat stroke or not enough water or something," she said to him. The boy exchanged a look with Janet, like they both had an idea of what the "or something" might be. "I know you just started a fifteen, but do you think you could take it later and fill in his spot until Ava comes in at two?"

The guy didn't pause to think about it. He simply stepped out of line with a nod and a "No problem." He was already moving to the slide station Janet had gestured at before she had a chance to exhale her temporary relief.

"Janet!" I called to her before she hustled off.

She jerked to a stop, glancing back. "Everything going okay here?" she asked, sounding doubtful, like she was waiting for me to walk out on her.

"Yeah. Great," I said. "That guy who you were talking to. The lifeguard." I nodded in his general direction. "Who is he?"

Janet almost smiled. I wasn't sure if it was relief I wasn't quitting or if it had something to do with the guy. "That's Quentin."

When she tried leaving again, I continued, "Does he work here, you know, all the time? Or is he just here helping for the day?" I didn't realize I'd crossed my fingers until I reached out to take the money from the next kid in line.

"He works here," she said with a little laugh, like that should have been obvious. "He's the head lifeguard."

My fingers uncrossed as I slumped forward on the counter. Of course he was.

Janet hustled away. Before I had a minute to fully appreciate just how much luck was messing with me, the door burst open and in flew a ball of dark hair and accessories.

"Sorry I'm late. Thirty-year-old cars and scorching-hot weather don't play well together." The girl hung her colorful tote on the side of the chip rack, raking at her disheveled hair before wrestling it into a high bun.

I must have been staring because she paused in the middle of her bun-making. "I'm Zoey, one of your fellow purgatory residents." Her eyes scanned the inside of the stand.

"Hey. I'm Jade."

"You could be a serial killer and I'd still be happy to meet you, Jade."

"Thanks?"

She spit her gum into the garbage can. "We were desperate for another concession employee."

"Glad it all worked out."

She paused, giving me a solid once-over. "You're not really a serial killer, though, are you?"

I fought a smile as I motioned to the next person in line. "Um, no."

Zoey was digging through her tote, looking more frustrated with every shovel of her hand. "Great. Awesome. I forgot my phone at home again. That's twice this week." Her collection of bracelets was jingling as she searched another second before giving up.

When I noticed the chipped black nail polish, matched with the forgetfulness and upfront approach, I couldn't help smiling. Add another fifteen years to her and a more edgy look and I'd have a Meg Abbott clone as a coworker.

"You can use mine if you need to make any calls. I don't mind." I freed my phone from my back pocket, setting it on the back counter.

"Really?"

"Of course."

"Nice, too?" Zoey appraised me with warm eyes as she adjusted a clutter of necklaces that had gotten tangled. "We're going to be good friends, Jade. I can already tell."

She was wearing a pair of scuffed-up motorcycle boots. In the dead of summer. She wouldn't have been the only one— Mom lived in boots in the summer. "I can, too," I said.

The hours that followed passed exactly like the hours before. Scooping buckets of ice cream, shaking out wrist cramps, exchanging money, and biting my tongue when the only part of the English vocabulary these pool piranhas didn't know was *please* and *thank you*. Having Zoey there made a huge difference, though. She whipped around that stand at warp speed, jingling and jangling as she went.

There was only one way the past few hours were different—

him. I couldn't *not* notice him. The harder I tried, the worse it became, until I eventually gave up and didn't berate myself for glancing in his direction every couple of minutes. He seemed entirely different from the person I'd exchanged "words" with yesterday. Serious, focused, and not a hint of amusement settling into his expression. He was more adult than boy out there on the pool deck, more parental than the parents relaxing in the loungers around him.

He took his job seriously, which I supposed was a good thing since, you know, people's lives were at stake. Compared to the other lifeguards, who were your typical teenage guys counting down the minutes until their shifts were over, he had something else going on. And he barely seemed to notice the flock of girls who magically congregated in his general vicinity. I didn't miss the way some of the moms were checking him out, either.

Right as I was about to take an order, I heard another whistle blow, but this one wasn't like the others I'd been hearing all day. This one was loud and sharp, getting every last person's attention in the pool area, from the young mom with Beats tucked over her ears to Janet, who was on a call in the office.

My eyes jumped to where I'd heard the sound, right in time to notice Quentin dive into the water like his life was on the line. Or someone's life was on the line.

The other guards at their posts started waving the rest of the swimmers out of the pool as Janet came bursting from the office. Zoey flew up beside me at the counter, shoving her red sunglasses on top of her head.

Everything got really quiet right then. I craned my neck to

see what was going on, and that was when Quentin emerged on the surface with another head in front of him. It looked like a little boy, but it was hard to tell from here. Suddenly, a shriek pierced the silence as a mom went streaking toward the end of the pool.

One of the other guards grabbed the kid to pull him from the water once Quentin made it to the edge. Quentin leaped out a half second after, kneeling to check on the boy, who was coughing a little but standing and breathing.

My heart was thumping out of control. I couldn't imagine how Quentin must have felt or the poor kid's mother. The boy looked like he'd had the poop scared out of him, but he was okay. No CPR or ambulances or—God, I hadn't really considered this yet—coroners needed.

Quentin was talking to the boy, checking him over as the mother inspected her son with anxious eyes like she was half-expecting to find a limb missing.

Leaning in, Quentin said something to the kid before raising his hand in the air. The boy answered with a high five before being guided away by his mom, who was talking with Janet. The lifeguard beside Quentin then pulled him over, pointing to his sunglasses now sunk at the bottom of the pool.

I couldn't help but stare as Quentin dove back into the water to retrieve them.

"And I thought I was hot before watching that." Zoey fanned her face with her hand, not blinking as she stared at Quentin.

"That was . . . ," I started.

"Insanely sexy?"

"Heroic. That's more what I was going for."

"Yeah, but insanely sexy works, too, right?" Zoey nudged me, giving me a knowing smile before getting back to opening a giant can of cheese sauce.

I was still staring at the spot where Quentin had disappeared into the water. The next kid in line started waving his cash at me, but I kept watching the pool.

When Quentin's head broke above the surface this time, he was looking in this direction. Well, actually, he was looking in *my* direction. It didn't matter that I had sunglasses on; he knew I was staring at him. And he made it clear that he was staring at me.

A slow smile lifted into place, one side higher than the other, and then he winked.

He winked.

What in the world was I supposed to do with that after yesterday?

A wink.

I wasn't sure if that was his way of making peace or declaring war, but I knew that either way, this boy would be a battle every step of the way.

Chapter Seven

He was hanging around after his shift and I wasn't sure why. He'd left his post on the deck at four, and when I guessed he was ready to peel out of the parking lot as fast as he could, he came meandering back, moving down a long line of empty loungers until he settled on what must have been exactly the right one.

I tried not to give much thought to why that happened to be the one directly across from the concession stand. Or why it felt like he'd lift his head every once in a while and glance at me through the cover of his sunglasses while I returned the look through the cover of mine.

And I definitely tried not to notice the way he stretched out on that lounger, too, with his long legs dangling off the end of the too-small chair, his skin seeming to tan before my eyes, and how his stupid shorts that clearly needed to have the elastic replaced wouldn't stop inching down lower whenever he moved.

For all I knew, he had no other plans than working on his tan and relaxing after a long shift, but as the time kept ticking by, I guessed his intentions had something to do with screwing with my head as well.

Mission accomplished.

Around five, there were only a few stragglers left in the pool, and the concession line had finally come to an end. Zoey had taken off a few minutes earlier, so I used that time to start cleaning up, but it didn't take long before that was done and I wasn't sure what to do. So I stood there, leaning into the counter, trying to ignore a boy who would not be forgotten.

When he finally did get up from the lounger a little while before closing, I could feel my lungs deflate with relief. Talk about awkward tension. One day down, and surely we wouldn't be working all the same shifts this summer.

Trouble, trouble, trouble, I started to sing to myself again. *T-R-O-U-B-L-E.*

Trouble, trouble. "Trouble." I didn't know I'd said it out loud until I noticed the look on his face change.

My hand shot over my mouth, like I was trying to take it back.

"Just one of my many nicknames," he said, already recovered. "But Quentin was the name I was given at birth, you know, before I went and created all of those nicknames for myself." That tipped smile went back into place, but he wasn't wearing sunglasses anymore. Nope. This time he was looking at me. Through me.

I kept my own glasses firmly in place.

"Let me guess, another one is Self-Absorbed? Delusional? Narcissistic?" Maybe I should have clamped my hand over my mouth again, but I'd never been big on censorship—of myself especially.

"You can add Crabby When Sleep-Deprived, Prone to Idiocy When Woken Up by a Pretty Girl, and Not Above Apologizing When I Was an Asshole."

His speech struck me silent. At least for a few seconds. "You accused me of gawking at you."

"How would you respond if you woke up to find some guy staring . . . *looking* at you inside your car?"

I reached for a towel to wipe the counter, needing a distraction. "I wouldn't have reacted like that. I wouldn't have accused someone of gawking at me. I'm not that in love with myself."

His smile held as he leaned into the counter. I slid down to the other end of it to clean. "What would you have done, then?"

My shoulder lifted. "I probably would have called him a creeper or something, before whipping out my can of pepper spray."

That made him laugh. "That is so much better than what I went with."

I had to bite my lip to keep from smiling, because he had a point. There wasn't really any best way to react to waking up to find a stranger peeking in your car window.

"Of course, the natural response to that was to accuse her of checking you out, because what red-blooded girl wouldn't want to check you out while you were snoring, drooling, and sweating inside your truck?" I said, playing along.

"Glad we got that cleared up." He folded his arms as he

leaned farther across the counter. I wished he'd put a shirt on, already.

"I'm not sure if we cleared up anything or made it more confusing, but sure." I glanced at the clock on the wall. Fifteen minutes to go. I'd have to find something else to clean because if I kept wiping at this same patch of counter, I was going to rub a dent in it. "But since we kind of work together, maybe we should forget about it and move on?"

"I like the way you think. Let's have a do-over." Gliding down the counter, he stuck his hand toward me. "Hi, I'm Quentin. I lifeguard here and frequently spend my breaks inside of my truck, sleeping."

I hesitated a moment too long to shake his hand. His smile shifted into a smirk. "Hey. I'm—"

"Jade." He lifted his chin. "I asked Janet."

"Oh."

My hand dropped back at my side. "Are you going to let me finish my end of the introduction?" I waited. He drew a zipper across his lips. "Hi, I'm Jade," I started again. "I just started working here as a concession employee, and if I actually got a break today, I could tell you what I prefer to do on mine."

"You didn't get a break today?"

"Unless you count that two minutes I chugged a bottle of water, then no, I didn't get a break."

"Yeah, the concession positions are the worst. Never enough people to work them. Can't keep anyone longer than a few weeks. If you'd asked me first, I would have told you to run away. Fast."

"I was too busy running away from you."

He made an O shape with his mouth, giving a mini wince. His expression cleared a half second later. "Hey, next time give me a shout and we'll coordinate our breaks. I'll cover concessions on one of my fifteens so you can at least get a few minutes to eat or whatever."

"Or catch up on my sleep?"

He nodded once, his eyes flashing. "Or that." The thought of food made my stomach grumble. Loud enough he could hear it. His brows lifted, like another of his points was being proven. "Really, I mean it. I know my way around the concession stand."

I wasn't sure what to think of him offering to use one of his breaks to give me one of my own. I wasn't sure what to think of this whole interaction. Yesterday I couldn't get away from him fast enough, but today I was being drawn in by more than his nice-to-look-at exterior.

Which kind of made me wish yesterday back, because I wasn't looking to get mixed up in anything of a romantic nature this summer. Especially with a boy like this one— I'd always been into the brooding artist types, never the hot jock types. Not to mention, if there was one thing Mom had pounded into me, it was not getting serious with a guy until I reached senior citizen status. Still had a few more years to go.

He hit me with another of those smiles. Everything south of my neck felt like it was melting as I reconsidered my position on those hot jock types.

"So, now that I think I've properly apologized and we've

had a better second first meeting, can I give you my order? I'm starving." He rolled his fingers across the counter, scooting in front of the cash register.

While he pulled some money from his shorts, I worked on issuing myself a reality check. This boy wasn't here to flirt—he was here to get some food.

It was official: I was an idiot.

"Oh. Yeah. Of course," I said, like that was the natural reason he'd be here talking to me right now. "What would you like?"

Quentin's eyes narrowed, like he had to give this some serious consideration. "I'll have a hot dog with everything on it. Make that two hot dogs with everything. An order of nachos with extra cheese. A bag of Doritos, a large Mountain Dew." His head bobbed side to side as he studied the menu. "And a triple scoop in a bowl. Yeah, that should be good. I don't want to ruin my dinner."

"Is that all?" I blinked at him, sure he was messing with me.

"Now that you mention it, throw in a licorice rope, too." Dead. Serious.

I shook my head as I started to make the hot dogs. "What flavors of ice cream?"

"Can I get two scoops of rocky road in one dish, and a to-go dish with a scoop of strawberry?" He waited, like he wasn't sure if I was going to agree. If he thought his request was outrageous, he had no idea what type of day I'd had.

"No problem. Your dessert after dinner?" I guessed as I moved on to loading up the nachos with a pool of cheese.

"Nah. I'm saving it for someone who's under the impression strawberry ice cream is the best thing ever."

I nodded, assuming he was referring to a girlfriend. *Taken*. Another cautionary word to beat into my brain before I started gawking at his lickable abs again.

"I probably should not be telling you this, since, you know, playing it cool is so much more the 'thing to do,' but I've never been very good at following the crowd." He rolled his neck, like he was pumping himself up for something. "I've kind of been hanging around all afternoon waiting for you to come say hey and make the next move."

The bag of Doritos I'd grabbed from the chip rack tumbled from my hand. "The *next* move?"

"You know, since I made the first. I thought it was your turn." He had no problem staring straight at me as he admitted all of this, which would be kind of endearing and refreshing if it wasn't so bewildering. "Instead, I made the first move, and now the second. Totally playing it cool over here."

When I was kneeling down to retrieve the Doritos, I felt safe enough to reply. Since I was able to think now that I wasn't looking at him. "What was the first move?"

He tapped the top of his head where a pair of sunglasses were settled. Then he pointed at the ones on the top of mine.

My stomach lurched. "*You* left these? You wrote the note?"

He gave me a funny look. "Of course I did. Who did you think it was?"

"I don't know. Someone else?"

"Someone else here who owed you an apology? How many cars did you stare into yesterday?" His gaze swept across the almost-empty pool area.

"One!" I laughed. "Well, thank you. That was . . ." I

struggled for the right word, sure the one I'd arrived at couldn't be right.

"*Nice?*" he suggested. "That was nice that I loaned you my good glasses while I wore my spare piece-of-crap ones? That's the word you're looking for, I think."

My eyes narrowed when I heard him yank the very word from my mouth. "Unexpected. That was more the word I was going for," I replied.

He lifted his eyes like he knew I was lying as I started to stack his feast in front of him. He tore into the bag of Doritos and tossed one into his mouth. "I'm really a pretty 'nice' guy," he said as he crunched on his chip. When he held the bag my way, I shook my head. "You can ask around if you don't believe me."

"You have a list of references, do you?" I glanced at him as I started ringing up his order.

His smile tipped into the realm of a grin. "I've got a whole telephone book of references."

"Of course you do. An all-female telephone book of 'nice' references." My fingers hovered above the keys, frozen like my brain.

"There's some dudes in there, too. Like the one I saved earlier from meeting a premature death. He'd probably be a pretty great reference as to my nice qualification."

"You did your job and saved his life. This makes you nice, how, exactly?"

Quentin exhaled. "Nothing's going to be easy with you, is it?"

The corners of my mouth started to pull up. "No, nothing's going to be easy with me."

Those green eyes of his felt like they were pushing me away at the same time they were pulling me closer. "Good," he said. "I like a challenge."

I returned his stare, proving I wasn't going to be flustered by a dreamy look and a few pointed words.

When his phone rang a moment later, our eyes roamed in other directions. Mine to the till, where I'd magically remembered how to ring up an employee order, while his latched onto the screen on his phone.

"What's up?" he answered, taking a sip of his soda. His face fell a moment later. "Did you check behind the hamper? Under my bed? Maybe it got kicked down into the sheets—" Whoever was on the other end cut him off. "Yeah, I'll be right there. I'm the master at unearthing Mr. Snuggles."

I had to bite my lip to keep from smiling, hearing him say "Mr. Snuggles."

After he ended the call, he started wrestling all his food into his arms. "Gotta run. Family emergency."

"Does it have anything to do with Mr. Snuggles?" I grinned at him as I balanced the half-eaten bag of Doritos on top of the food pyramid.

"The little bastard has gone MIA again, and I'm the only one in the house who is apparently qualified to find him."

"Good luck, soldier," I said solemnly as I took his ten-dollar bill and started to make change, but he was already striding away. "Your change!" I called.

"Hit me up tomorrow, okay?"

I clutched the dollar and coins in my fist. "This doesn't have anything to do with some evil plan of yours to force me to make the third move, does it?"

He spun around, a wide smile on his face as he continued to back away toward the exit. "Of course it does."

"I thought you liked a challenge."

Like he had in the pool earlier, he flashed another wink at me. "I thought you did, too."

Chapter Eight

I was starting to understand why Aunt Julie wanted to spend every waking minute with me: because her husband didn't seem to spend a single one with her.

Okay, so maybe that was an exaggeration, but only slightly. This was my fourth night in the Davenport house, and I'd run into him a total of three times. Four if you count the time we passed in the hall early this morning as he was rushing off to the office. The guy had a work ethic, but it was the kind that didn't leave much room for anything else, including my aunt, who I was starting to believe was the loneliest human being I'd ever met.

"How's dinner? It's my first attempt at veggie noodles, and I'm not sure I got them quite right." Across the table from me, Aunt Julie was scrutinizing her plate like all she saw was a pile of flaws and failures. On either side of her were my cousins, sitting perfectly straight in their seats, napkins poised in their laps, eating their meals like they were dining with dignitaries. I felt like a pig at the trough in comparison.

"It's amazing," I said, twirling another bite onto my fork.

"The noodles are perfect and the sauce is so good I want to take a bath in this stuff." I glanced at the girls for confirmation, who dutifully nodded.

Aunt Julie stopped examining her plate long enough to smile up at me. "It's coconut curry. I thought you might enjoy it."

"Oh, believe me, I am." Most of my dinner was already gone, while she had yet to touch hers, but that had been the trend at dinner lately. Those breaks I was supposed to get at work had a way of never actually happening.

So I ate both lunch and dinner at dinnertime.

Quentin was supposed to work yesterday, but there'd been some kind of family emergency, so one of the on-call guards covered for him (turns out that is a thing!), and today he had off. It wasn't like I was disappointed I hadn't seen him in a couple of days, but I still had his change and wanted to get it to him. All one dollar and seventy-two cents of it.

Aunt Julie was lifting her first bite of veggie pasta to her mouth when the front door opened. The sound of Uncle Paul's dress shoes echoing on the wood floors grew louder until he was in the dining room.

Aunt Julie started peeling the plastic wrap from his dinner plate at the head of the table and pouring him a glass of white wine. The twins smiled at their dad as he rounded the table, but he barely noticed. "How was work, sweetie?"

Uncle Paul patted the top of the twins' heads as he passed, his standard greeting and good-bye. "Busy," he replied, pulling off his tie before he started to stack silverware on his plate. Aunt Julie's face fell. "I've got to prep for my morning meetings, so do you mind if I take dinner into my office?" he asked, already leaving the room.

Aunt Julie worked up her most convincing smile. "Of course not. Let me know if you need anything."

Uncle Paul bit a chunk of his roll off as he continued away. "You're the best, babe." His voice was muffled as he chewed. "Good day at camp, girls?"

They nodded at the same time, Hannah opening her mouth like she was about to tell a story, but Uncle Paul missed it. "Good day at work, Jade?"

His footsteps were echoing away, when I replied, "Worst day ever."

Aunt Julie shot me a surprised look, so I shook my head. It wasn't, but I was trying to prove a point.

"Glad to hear it." Uncle Paul's voice came from somewhere down the hall before the sound of his office door closing.

Dinner was a silent affair after that, Aunt Julie scooting food around on her plate but not really eating any of it, her eyes occasionally wandering toward the empty seat at the end of the table. The girls finished up their meals, asked to be excused, cleared their plates, then left to start getting ready for bed.

"Do you mind if I head to the park tonight? Before it gets dark," I added, getting better at anticipating Aunt Julie's next questions and concerns before she voiced them.

"What are you going to do at the park? Are you meeting anyone there?" She started to clear the pretty setting she'd put out for tonight's dinner.

"I'm not meeting anyone; I just felt like chilling there and reading for a while. It looks like a nice park." I biked past it on my way to work, and one of the big trees on the perimeter would be a perfect spot to lounge and either read or write, depending on my mood.

"Alone? I don't know, Jade. . . ."

"It's only two blocks away, Aunt Julie, and I'll have my phone on me. I'll be home before dark, I promise." I finished my last bite and started to help her clear. "I'll stay out of trouble."

The way I said it made her smile at the same time that she lifted a parental-type brow. "And what if trouble finds you?"

My nose wrinkled as I shook my head. "I repel trouble."

As we carried our plates into the kitchen, I was prepared to bring up the fact that I was a seventeen-year-old requesting permission to go to a park to read on a Friday night, in case she voiced any other hesitations, but there was no need.

"I suppose it's okay," she said with a sigh, like she'd signed away my life. "Please make sure you're home before dark. We're responsible for you this summer, and I don't want your mom to think we're letting you run wild."

I had to bite the inside of my cheek to keep from telling her that if she thought tonight's request was running wild, she'd drop if she knew about the time I'd stayed out all night riding a bike around the streets of Seville, Spain, when the Shrinking Violets performed a few concerts there two summers ago.

Not that it was "wild" behavior—no boys or booze had been involved—but I knew I had more freedom than most teenage girls.

"Thanks, Aunt Julie," I said as I turned on the hot water to start rinsing the dishes.

"I've got this tonight," she said, scooting me aside to take my place. "Go enjoy your reading time."

"Are you sure? I don't mind helping."

"You worked a full day and fixed the leaky kitchen faucet. Go be a teenager, for crying out loud." She nudged me and glanced at the door.

"Don't worry. I won't be one of those teenagers who makes the evening news or anything." I gave her a quick hug. Aunt Julie froze for a moment—then she relaxed. "Thanks for an awesome dinner. I'm sure Uncle Paul's loving it, too."

Her face went just sad enough for me to catch. "I'm sure."

As I headed up the stairs to grab my stuff, I fought the urge to step into Uncle Paul's office. He was a good guy, and I knew he took his work seriously, but Aunt Julie and the girls shouldn't come second. I should say something to him—once I figured out how to say it. I added it to my summer to-do list as I gathered up *Jane Eyre* and my journal and shot back down the stairs to take advantage of the last couple hours of light.

Once I'd made it through the front door, I heaved a sigh of relief. Other than the short walk I'd taken last night after dinner, this was the only time I'd been out on my own when I wasn't heading either to or from work. I'd missed my freedom, and feeling it now made my wanderlust stir.

I couldn't wait to get to the park. I'd left off at one of my favorite parts of the book, and I wanted to dive back in. I started reading as I wandered down the quiet sidewalk.

It was the perfect kind of night. Warm but not hot, just enough breeze to play with the billowy layers of my tunic and the ends of my hair, and my feeling that this sidewalk led anywhere I wanted it to. Whether it be the park another block and a half away or the edge of the Pacific Ocean, every road led somewhere. Some roads led everywhere. Mom taught me that.

"Hi, neighbor," a familiar voice called to me across the yard I was wandering by, my nose in my book.

My feet stuck to the sidewalk. It couldn't be. No way.

When I peeked over, I found him grinning at me from the top step of the front porch. I gathered myself before replying. "You say this like you knew we were neighbors."

Nice. Totally chill-sounding.

His shoulders lifted beneath the faded gray tee he had on. So he did have clothes—jeans and everything. "I did."

"When did you find out?"

"A few nights ago. The same night after we'd had our, you know, 'misunderstanding' in the parking lot." He sat up, resting his elbows on his bent legs.

"When did you see me?" I scanned my memory, but the only time I'd been outside was heading to and from the pool on Lemon-the-kinda-bike.

"When you were sitting in one of the windows facing the street. It was pretty late." He said this all matter-of-factly, like he was reading a weather report instead of confessing he'd been watching me through my bedroom window late at night.

I lowered my book. "You were spying on me?"

His hand rubbed at his mouth, probably trying to hide his twitching smile. "Seemed only fair, since you spied on me."

My throat went dry when I thought of what he might have seen through my bedroom window. "What did you see?"

His eyes didn't dodge me as he answered, "Just some girl reading." He paused, clearing his throat. "And maybe crying as she read a letter."

I was relieved he hadn't seen me trotting around in my underwear, but at the same time I was furious he'd seen me so vulnerable. "I can't believe you."

He didn't look the least bit fazed by my outrage. "So who wrote the note? Some loser who broke your heart?"

My weight shifted. I wasn't expecting this detour into a spying-neighbor confession. "No boy's ever made me cry. And one's certainly never broken my heart."

"Why? Don't have one of those four-chamber things in your chest?"

I narrowed my eyes at him, even though I was kind of enjoying our banter. "Because I've never let one get close enough to my heart to break it."

Quentin nodded. "That's a guaranteed way to protect yourself from a heartbreak." He paused, a strange look settling on his face. "And love," he added as an afterthought.

"Family emergency under control now?" I asked, taking a moment to inspect the yard. I hadn't noticed it at first, since I'd been a little shocked discovering that Quentin and I were almost next-door neighbors, but there were more toys scattered around the yard than actual organic matter. Everything from footballs and soccer goals to a turtle sandbox and a stroller.

"All under control," he answered, checking something he was holding in his hand. "Thanks for asking."

When I noticed a stuffed elephant dangling from the stroller, it made me think of something. "How's Mr. Snuggles?"

Quentin's chest lifted with a huff. "Being snuggled as we speak." When he lifted his hand, he was holding a baby monitor, and on the screen I spotted a baby asleep in a crib, a stuffed bear tucked close by.

"My parents are out, so I'm in charge," he explained, his eyes softening when he checked the monitor screen. Which made my heart go kind of soft, too.

"Girl or boy?" I asked, motioning at the baby.

"Girl. Lily's her name."

"And I'm going to guess she's the only girl in the house?" I swept my arm toward the yard, where the most "girl" toy was . . . the purple lightsaber-looking thing.

Quentin grumbled when he inspected the mess scattered around the yard. "Two younger devils. Or 'brothers,' when my mom's in hearing range."

Okay, so this guy wasn't only the head lifeguard at the public pool, he also babysat his three younger siblings. The more I got to know Quentin, the more I realized how many sides he had.

"My parents will be home by nine. Want to hang out later?" he asked.

When I stayed quiet, he prodded, "Yes or no. Those are the most common answers to that kind of a question. You know, in case you were wondering."

"What did you have in mind?" I shifted again, not sure why this boy made me so uncomfortable. One minute he made me feel like I should steer clear, only to fight the urge to come closer the next.

He set the monitor down and clasped his hands together, grinning up at me. "I've got plans."

That was what I was worried about.

"What *type* of plans?"

Quentin grinned. "The good type." He let that hang between us before continuing. "Better ones than spending the summer reading books in the park." His knuckles tapped the cover of my book, almost like he was knocking on some door he was waiting for me to answer.

"I like books," I replied, all brilliant-like.

He gave me a look.

"I *love* books," I added, holding his unblinking stare. He was trying to make a point—so was I.

"Why don't you try creating your own story instead of living inside the pages of someone else's imagination?"

I was ready to argue back, but I hadn't been expecting him to say that. I hadn't been ready for him to call me out for almost the same thing Mom had in her letter. Sure, his delivery was filled with more accusation than hers, but the takeaway was the same—live *your* life.

"You don't know me," I said slowly, taking a step back. "Just because I love books doesn't mean I don't have a life."

"You're right. I don't know you. But I'd like to." His eyes squinted when he looked up at me, the evening sun glinting down on him.

"Why?" I asked.

He stood, rising slowly from his perch on the steps, walking down a step, and then another, until he was standing on the same level as I was. "Because." He stuffed his hands into his jeans pockets and shrugged.

"Why?"

He moved a step closer, hesitated for a moment, then

took one more. His eyes found mine. "Because I think you're worth knowing."

Tingles crawled down my back. Actual tingles.

"Maybe another time," I said, backing toward the sidewalk.

"I know the definition of maybe." He took his own step back toward the porch. "Never."

I paused when I hit the sidewalk. "I'll think about it, okay?"

He waved, still moving away. "Don't think about it for too long. Or summer will be over."

His words were a challenge, a dare. That's all I could think about as I finished my trek to the park. By the time I was stretched out under the tree I'd scoped out a few days ago, I was restless. I couldn't get comfortable, the bark rubbing my back wrong, the roots beneath me prodding my backside.

I was too aggravated to even think about writing, but I found the same problem waiting for me when I opened my book. I couldn't make it through one paragraph without replaying Quentin's and my conversation.

No wonder I'd just read the same page for the ninth time and still hadn't processed it.

Slamming down my book with a grumble, I heard my phone chime in my pocket. Usually I was annoyed when I got a call during reading or writing time, but this one was a welcome distraction.

"Mom!" I answered.

"Daughter!" she greeted back.

"Oh my gosh, what time is it in London?" I sat up, trying to calculate the difference.

"Time to call you. That's what time it is." She didn't sound tired, despite it being probably 4 A.M.

"I miss you. How are things?" I wasn't sure where the tears came from, but I suddenly felt them burning the surface of my eyes. Thanks to her schedule and time zone issues, we'd only gotten to exchange texts and emails since she left.

"I miss you more because I'm the mom and that's my right, but things are going pretty darn great tour-wise. They'd be going even better if you were here, because I swear to God, Jade, you were a better stage manager at fifteen than these supposed professionals. Last night, they set my acoustic guitar out for the opening set, you know, instead of that electric one I kind of need to rock 'Wallflower Flunkie.'"

Hearing her voice made me smile. "What did you do?"

"We played the first-ever acoustic version of 'Wallflower Flunkie.' The crowd went berserk. It was killer. You would have loved it."

I laughed as I pictured the scene, plucking at the frayed hems of my cutoffs. "What are you going to be playing acoustic next? 'Rebel Honey'?"

Mom laughed on the other end. "I like it, Jade. I'll have to run it by Seraphina and Kai. See what they think."

"Tell them hey for me. And remind Kai that she needs to order new guitar picks. She's got to be running low."

"I'll do both," Mom promised. "Enough about me, what have you been up to?" She paused, like she was waiting for me to start rattling off a whole checklist of things. "What are you doing right at this very moment?"

I glanced down at my book and journal before scanning the park for something I could tell her that didn't involve admitting I was reading a book I'd already read ten dozen times.

"Right this very moment?" I said, hoping it would buy me another minute to come up with something genius.

"Jade Eleanor Abbott. If you are reading one of those books of yours on a Friday night all by your lonesome, I am going to haul my ass to the airport and catch the first flight to California."

Okay, so this really wasn't the right time to tell her what I'd been up to. "Mom—"

"Jade. Go. Do. Experience."

I plucked at the grass. "I've traveled to six continents and thirty-one countries and I'm still not even an adult in the eyes of the government. I have gone and done and experienced."

She was quiet for a moment, but I knew what she was getting at. Kind of. I'd done a lot in seventeen years of life, but I'd missed out on a lot, too. This was what this summer was all about, and here I was, reading under a tree like I would have been if I were currently in London with the Shrinking Violets.

"You don't have to worry about taking care of me or Seraphina or Kai, baby. We're big girls. I know you do a great job at it, but we can take care of ourselves, too. You don't have to worry about equipment or tour schedules or anything but being a seventeen-year-old." I heard noise in the background, but then what sounded like a door closing came next, and it was quiet again. "I want you to make friends and have fun and get into trouble." She stopped when she realized what she'd said. "A little trouble. Not too much, but some. I'm giving you my permission."

My head fell back into the tree. "I don't know the parameters for some trouble. Can you define it?"

"You'll know it when you feel it. You have good instincts."

"All right. I'll try."

"No, Jade Eleanor. You'll *do*."

Chapter Nine

After I hung up with Mom, I lingered under the tree for a few more minutes, giving everything a chance to settle. But then I got a text from her that read: *I'm en route to Heathrow. I know you've still got that book in your hand. I can feel it all the way across the Atlantic.*

Technically, the book wasn't in hand but beside me on the ground; however, mentioning that would only make her bribe the taxi to drive faster. So instead, I leaped up from the ground and collected my stuff, typing in a quick response so she knew my Friday night was on the move.

When I passed Quentin's house, I gave it a sideways look because just in case he was spying on me again, I didn't want him to know I was also spying on him. The clutter in the yard had been picked up, and no infuriating boys were stretched out on the porch steps. Dad and Mom must have been home for the night because there was an SUV in the driveway that hadn't been there before, but Quentin's truck was still there.

After I passed his place, my gaze wandered to my aunt and uncle's, where I could see something big and brown on the front porch that had not been there when I left. It was a box. A big one.

Maybe a late delivery or something.

As I headed up the walkway, though, I realized the box was open, and inside was a whole mess of worn paperback books. There was a note propped on top of the heap, so that's what I reached for first.

Enough to get you through the whole summer. Enjoy.

I didn't need to know who it was from—it was obvious. My head whipped toward Quentin's house, my blood warming when I started to shuffle through the heap of books. They were all romance novels. The ones with cheesy covers and silly titles displayed in enormous cursive letters.

My eyes narrowed. I didn't read those kinds of books. At all. Embarrassed, I tried wrestling the box through the doorway, but it was too heavy, so I wound up dragging it in behind me.

"Jade? Is that you?" Aunt Julie's voice chimed from the kitchen. "Did you see the present on the front porch?"

"It's a real gift," I mumbled, feeling like I was about to pull a muscle from dragging an elephant's weight of books a few feet.

"I would have brought it in, but Quentin said he wanted you to be surprised by finding it on the porch."

I was taken aback that Aunt Julie knew Quentin. It made sense—he did live down the block, after all. But their worlds felt so . . . different.

"It was quite the surprise. I can't wait to return the favor."

I was already scheming ways to pay him back. "So you know Quentin?" Aunt Julie would be on my side if anyone would. The loather of all things of a trouble-like nature would definitely be with me on this.

"A little, yeah, but I didn't know you knew him." She poked her head out of the kitchen. "He sure is a nice boy, Jade. Not so bad to look at, either."

"Not so great to look at, either," I muttered. Her side-eye made it apparent that lie was fooling no one. "Do you know his family or something?" I asked, to change the subject.

"We've exchanged waves and said hi, but no, I wouldn't say I know them or anything. They moved in about a year ago. They seem like a nice family, busy but nice. Then again, who wouldn't be busy raising that many kids? And with that big of an age gap." Aunt Julie shook her head and grimaced, like four kids ranging from baby to teenager under one roof was in the same vein as capital punishment.

I couldn't believe Aunt Julie didn't look at him and see a dozen different caution signs flashing above his head like I did. Then again, she wasn't worried about having her heart thrown into a shredder if she got too close.

"Hey, Aunt Julie?" I paused to make sure I had her attention. "How would you feel about me going out tonight?"

The look she gave me led me to the conclusion she didn't understand the question. "As in . . . *now*?"

"Yeah, maybe." I motioned at the front window.

"Where would you be going?"

I rolled my weight from my heels to the balls of my feet, not sure why I was asking when I probably already knew her answer. "I don't know. Somewhere."

"Alone? With someone?"

When I answered her with a raise of my shoulders, she braced her hands against the counter ledge. "What time do you plan on being back?"

"Um, I don't know. Is one an acceptable time?"

Her eyes went as round as they could. "One o'clock in the morning? I don't think so." When she saw me slump in front of her, she took a breath. "Listen, you're just getting settled in here. There's no reason for you to be going out 'somewhere' and not getting home until one."

"Mom used to let me," I replied, trying not to sound like I was whining.

Aunt Julie gave me one of those sad smiles, like it would somehow make the verdict easier to swallow. "Sweetie, I'm not your mom."

Didn't I know it?

Plastering on a smile of my own, I turned to go upstairs. "I'm heading up to my room. Do you mind if I leave the box of books in the foyer for the night?" There was no sense in dragging them upstairs when I had no intention of keeping them.

"That's fine. Have a good night." Aunt Julie lifted her hand from the sandwich she was making for Uncle Paul's lunch and waved at me. She was still in her slacks and blouse, her hair and makeup looking as fresh as they had this morning.

"See you in the morning," I said, jogging up the stairs, adrenaline pumping in my veins as my plan started to hatch. Quentin had thrown down the gauntlet, and I wasn't the type who walked away from a challenge. He was daring me, calling me out, knowing I wouldn't rise to the occasion—I'd show him he didn't have any idea what kind of girl I was.

Shutting my door behind me, I moved across the room to the window and opened it. It didn't open all noisy and creaky like most of the windows I'd crawled through. I should have known Aunt Julie's windows would be streak- *and* squeak-free.

After turning off all my lights, I changed from my cutoffs and tunic and into a flowy knee-length dress. I wasn't sure why I was going with a dress when I'd be climbing from a window and taking part in some TBD adventure tonight, but it was the first thing I'd reached for.

Not sure if Aunt Julie would stick her head into my room tonight—I really hoped she wouldn't—but just in case . . .

Grabbing a few pillows from the window seat, I stuffed them under the blankets on my bed until I'd created a pillow teenager sound asleep beneath the covers.

Stepping back to inspect what I'd done, my stomach curled into knots. I hated the idea of going behind Aunt Julie's back and sneaking out, but this was the only way I was going to get to experience real, true teenage life, since Aunt Julie treated me like a toddler who had to be monitored at all times. I was responsible and made good choices—I'd proven that my whole life—and my actual parent had never minded when I'd crawled out of windows or explored the city alone. In fact, she would encourage it.

The window was huge—made for climbing from—and the distance from the roof to the ground was nothing compared to other heights I'd jumped from. I jogged across the dark yard. The lights were still on downstairs, but it was getting close to ten, which was bedtime. Aunt Julie was as meticulous about that aspect of her life as she was about the others.

Quentin's house was quiet as I approached, his truck still parked in the driveway. My heart was hammering in my chest, seeming to echo into the quiet night. I felt the rush of the unexpected, the thrill of doing something I probably shouldn't have been, and the dread of what would happen as a result. It was a strong mix of emotions sweeping through me, but I liked it. A lot.

Since I wasn't sure what time he was planning on leaving for the night, I took a seat on his bumper. I couldn't wait to see the look on his face when he found me here.

I didn't have to wait long.

It wasn't a window that whined open but a front door. He didn't rush away like he was worried about getting caught; he bounced down the stairs and loped across the yard like he wasn't worried about anyone seeing him leave. Maybe his parents were cool with him heading out at night.

He didn't see me at first. Not until I'd stood up and come around the side of his truck. When he noticed me, a smile slipped into place, his eyes flashing like he'd been expecting me all along.

He turned to face me, leaning into the driver's door. "So you didn't like your present?"

My mouth twitched as I moved closer. "I hated it."

"Good." Saying nothing else, he opened his door and motioned me inside.

"Nice dress." His words matched the appraisal in his eyes.

I tugged at the hem, wondering why I felt so self-conscious. Maybe it had something to do with the way he was looking at me. "I wasn't sure what you had in mind for the night, but hopefully it's dress-appropriate."

"Totally." He didn't step aside as I crawled into his truck, so my shoulder brushed across his chest. Which meant I felt like a million volts had just shot through my rotator cuff. "My plan was to hang upside down on the monkey bars all night, so really, you couldn't have picked a better outfit."

I rolled my eyes as I scooted across the bench seat.

As I buckled up, I glanced into the backseat. It was in the same condition as his yard had been earlier. Foam nunchakus, plastic dinosaurs, and a car seat.

When Quentin climbed in, he saw me checking out the back. He lifted his chin as he fired up the truck. "That's how I roll."

He said it like he was the epitome of cool, making me laugh. "I've never seen a car seat in a teenage guy's car. Or a Captain America shield, for that matter," I said, noticing a few more items scattered across the floor in back.

Quentin's forehead creased. "You know? I haven't either. Must mean I'm a rare breed. One of those one-in-a-billion types."

He backed out of the driveway slowly, checking his mirrors more than once. He was a responsible driver, which gave me hope we weren't heading to some kind of satanic rave in an abandoned warehouse tonight.

"You really like yourself, don't you?" I said.

"Hey, I'm a great guy. There's a lot to like."

When he caught me rolling my eyes after he put the truck in drive, he said, "Okay, so you're one of those girls who's into the self-loathers." He tapped his hand against the steering wheel, thinking. His shoulders fell at the same time his expression went dark and brooding. "No, I don't like myself.

At all. I'm a piece of crap, deserving of nothing. I don't know why anyone could ever like a parasite like me. I want to lock myself in a dark room and listen to dark music and contemplate dark things." When he peered over at me, I grumbled and shook my head.

He had a comeback for everything. Instead of confirming or denying what "kind of girl" I was and what "kind of guy" I liked, I stayed silent. His truck wasn't so quiet, though. It was loud—not one of those designed to make noise, but more as if it was approaching its expiration date.

"You're one of those boho chics, eh? Keeping Urban Outfitters in business?" Quentin glanced over at my dress as we headed down the street.

"What's Urban Outfitters?" I asked, pulling at the hem again. "And what's a boho chic?"

"You know." He nodded. "Someone who dresses like you."

I glanced down at my dress, my sandals, my fringy crossbody purse. No idea what he was talking about. "I shop at thrift stores and the occasional vintage shop."

He shrugged again, like I was confirming his point. "Boho chic."

I twisted in my seat so I was facing him. "Yeah, if you ever try calling me a boho chic again, I'm going to dump that pile of books you left me on your head."

He grinned at the windshield. "No labels?"

"No thank you."

"Why not?" he asked, turning down onto a busy main road.

"Because labels confine you. They don't let you move outside of them. We labelless nuts of the world can be whoever we want, whenever we want." I rolled down my window a little, feeling like I needed the fresh air. That might have had to do with how good he smelled, all wet-haired and fresh from the shower.

"Sounds nice."

"It is," I replied.

A couple of minutes passed as we continued down the road to our mystery destination. I could have asked, but he probably wouldn't have told me, and really, I didn't want to know.

"So. The story. What's yours?" Quentin asked as he turned onto the street that ran along the ocean. It was the first time I'd seen the ocean since getting here, and I felt like a kid rolling down the window so I could stick my head out and smell the night. The air wasn't so briny down here like it was along the Washington and Oregon coasts, but it still had that nice sea smell.

"Which one?" I asked, surfing my arm through the window after I pulled my head back in.

"The all-encompassing one."

I stiffened as I thought about explaining that one. "Long story."

"They usually are." He turned into a big parking lot, managing to snag a spot up front that someone was leaving.

Were we going to the beach? As nice as that sounded, I'd be surprised if this was Quentin's big plan.

"Let's see." I tapped my chin as he parked. "I was born, I lived, and now I'm here. There's the end."

He snorted and turned off the engine. "Come on. Really?"

He spun in his seat so he was facing me. "Some girl suddenly moves in a few houses down from mine and I get no details?"

I blinked, debating how much to tell him. We didn't know each other, not really. The few conversations Quentin and I'd had were more focused on challenging or teasing each other than delving into our pasts. "The couple is my aunt and uncle, and I'm only here for the summer," I said, opening the door. He opened his, too. "Sorry. That's about as juicy as it gets."

Quentin was nodding as he met me around the front of his truck. "Wanted to check out the California coast during the summer?" His eyes lifted to the beach in front of us, like it was an explanation.

"Kind of," I started, not sure how much I wanted to explain. I definitely wasn't bringing up my birth father. "Mainly, I just wanted to spend a summer like everyone else my age."

His head cocked as he started down the wide walkway running along the beach. He only took a step before waiting to make sure I was following. "How have you spent your other summers?"

"Like I have the rest of my life. On the road. Traveling. Seeing the country. Visiting the world. That kind of thing."

His mouth hung open for a moment as he stared at me. "And you wanted a break from all of that traveling stuff because . . . ?"

The way he was looking at me made me smile. It was similar to the way my mom had gaped at me when I told her I wanted to spend the summer with Aunt Julie. "Because what if I was missing out on something?"

"What if you're missing out on *nothing*?" he argued as we wandered down the walkway.

"Then I'll know for sure come the end of August."

He was still shaking his head, like I was clinically crazy. "So? Where have you been?"

"It would be easier to list where I *haven't* been."

He groaned, like he was in pain. "You're killing me."

"What? Haven't you traveled?"

"Eh, yeah. To Phoenix to see my grandparents and Wisconsin to see my other grandparents. Whoop-de-do." He circled his index finger in the air. "Where's the best place you've ever been?"

"That's hard. I like lots of places."

"If you had to pick one place to spend the rest of your life, where would it be?"

My eyes narrowed as I considered that. I'd visited some crazy-beautiful places and seen a good chunk of the world, but nowhere felt like home.

"Why have you spent so much time traveling?" he continued when I stayed quiet. "Is your dad in the military or something?"

I didn't really "know" my dad, but what I did know of him made me almost laugh when I pictured him saluting in camos.

"No, definitely not. My mom's in a band, so they travel a lot. They have a big international following, too, so we got to go all over, from Reykjavik to Sydney."

Quentin came to a stop. He grabbed my arm when I kept going. "Your mom's in a band?"

"Yeah," I answered, like she was no different from moms who rolled up to carpool lines in minivans.

"Is this a band I've heard of?" He wasn't letting go of my arm. I wasn't sure I wanted him to.

"That depends. Do you listen to grunge-meets-glam-chick-rock?" I failed to mention that if he ever listened to the Top 40, he probably would recognize a few of their hits.

"Yeah, I stick to classic rock, so probably not." His hand dropped away from my arm as he started walking again. "If you were on the road all the time, what did you do for school?"

"I was homeschooled." Up ahead was a big pier where a carnival had been set up. There was a Ferris wheel towering above the rest of the rides, and I could already smell the food and hear the game vendors challenging bystanders to become customers. He was taking me to a carnival? I loved carnivals. Every city in the world had one, and they were all the same—from Akron to Zagreb.

"Homeschooled, really? Wow," he said, pulling me out of my cotton-candy revelry.

"Yes. Explain the not-so-subtle surprise." I nudged his arm, giving him a look.

"I don't know. I guess I think of homeschooled kids as being socially inept or something. All of that being alone and not having other classmates to help build the thick skin all of us public schooled kids have by the time we reach second grade."

"Nah, I think the opposite is true. We have to try extra-hard and go out of our way to make friends and fit in. We're easily adaptable." I checked my phone in my purse to make sure I hadn't missed any frantic calls or texts from Aunt Julie, you know, in case she discovered the sleeping niece was really a strategically placed line of pillows. "So what about you? What's *your* life story?"

Quentin rubbed the back of his head, keeping his eyes forward. "Well, it isn't anything close to as cool as yours, that's for sure. My mom is currently a stay-at-home mom, not in a rock band. The most exotic place I've ever been is Baja, and I've gone to public schools since kindergarten."

"That's not a life story. That's just random facts."

When we came to the pier, he steered us toward it. "Well, neither was yours," he stated, carving a direct path to the closest fried food vendor he saw. "You want something to eat? I'm starving."

"Didn't you have dinner?"

"Yeah. Three hours ago." My face must have been blank because he went on to explain, "That's like an eternity to a growing boy."

"Unbelievable," I mumbled when I realized we were waiting in line at a fried ice cream vendor.

"What do you want? My treat." He had his wallet in his hand and was getting some money as we moved up in line.

"I want . . . not to be diagnosed with type two diabetes by the time I'm forty." I pointed at the menu, where the healthiest thing listed was fried strawberry cheesecake on a stick because, ya know, fruit.

Quentin suddenly spun and grabbed me by the shoulders, looking me dead in the eye as if we were discussing a matter of life and death. "Listen, Jade, we only have a small window of time to eat what we want and do what we want and be who we want before that all changes and we have to start thinking about cholesterol and regular bedtimes and turning into this mature, responsible model citizen. Live it up while you can."

"You seem to be living it up enough for the both of us." I laughed, as Quentin let go of me and listed off his order to the girl behind the register. He didn't hear me, though, because the girl had gotten his attention, asking him some question that I'm sure didn't have anything to do with his order. To be fair, any girl wearing a shirt that low and a bra that elevating was bound to garner some stares.

I stepped aside as they chatted it up and he waited for his fried feast on a stick. This wasn't a date, I reminded myself; this was hanging out. One coworker inviting another one out for a good time. This *wasn't* a date. But I found my jaw locking as she rubbed at his arm, laughing.

And she wasn't the only one giving Quentin the eye. A trio of girls in line behind him were not being discreet about what they thought of his posterior.

My stomach churned. Not with jealousy, I didn't think— I felt almost . . . protective of him. He was more than just a nice butt.

Not cool. Not cool at all. I needed to get my emotions in check before I started to think they meant something.

Once Quentin got his food, he waved good-bye to the girl and wandered over to where I was waiting. "Want a bite?" He held out the fried cheesecake, offering it to me first.

"No thanks."

"Live it up. . . ."

I rolled my eyes as he shook it in front of me. "Find me something vegan fried on a stick, and I'll try it, I promise."

He blinked at me. "You're vegan? Well, crap. If I'd known that, I would have gone for the fried-broccoli-on-a-stick stand on the other end."

"Fried broccoli on a stick. I bet the demand for something like that at a carnival is off the charts. Besides, the hippie dude manning the broccoli stand isn't nearly as stacked."

Quentin glanced over at me as we milled through the crowd, looking almost amused. "Stacked?" He repeated it like he'd never heard the term.

"Oh, please. Don't pretend your eyes weren't about to go crossed back there."

Quentin bit into his cheesecake. "I wasn't staring at her boobs, if that's what you're getting at."

His blunt word choice took me by surprise. "Then what were you staring at?"

Quentin was trying to keep from grinning, I could tell. "Her heart. Naturally."

"Uh," I groaned, shoving his arm.

"It was hidden from view. I had to look really, *really* close to see it." He took a bite of his cheesecake to keep from laughing. "Joking, joking." He raised his hands in surrender. "For your information, she's the girlfriend of one of my surfing buddies, Sam."

"Does Sam know how buddy-buddy you are?" I smirked.

He leaned in, unfazed. "Sam's a girl." He let that simmer for a minute, until he started to see the realization hit me.

"Oh." Another brilliant response from yours truly.

"Still have room to be surprised, do you, cultured world traveler?"

"Oh, shut up," I grumbled, which only made him chuckle. What was wrong with me? I was way off my game. Making assumptions, jumping to conclusions, acting like a possessive psycho.

"Games." He pointed.

"Those things are designed to take your money. The chance of actually winning something is slim to none," I said, nudging him with my arm. "At least for people like you who aren't carnival junkies."

Quentin was already handing over a five-dollar bill at one of the stands where you threw a baseball at some creepy-looking stuffed clowns to try to knock one over. "Why do I feel like you're making a habit of underestimating me?" he teased, tossing his first ball into the air and catching it. I was about to offer to hold his food when he started to wind up. His wild pitch made me step back.

One clown down. Two balls to go.

"Impressed?" He grinned over at me, reaching for his second ball.

"That you can throw a ball?"

He cocked his head, and then he fired his next throw. Two clowns down.

Okay, so I was semi-impressed. He was two for two.

"Now you're impressed."

"That you can throw a ball at a stationary target fifteen feet away?"

Tossing his hand into the air like I was impossible, he

picked up the third ball right after and sent it flying. Like, so hard I could hear it whizzing through the air.

Three clowns down.

"I'm not even going to ask if you're impressed this time." Quentin thanked the person who handed him his prize, a cute stuffed bear.

"Fast learner."

Quentin got back to his food, holding the bear out. "For you," he said. "I know, I know, you're not impressed by how I won it, but I'm pretty sure you girls still secretly love it when a guy wins you a cuddly toy."

Taking the bear, I dug my own five from my purse, heading toward the closest game. Which, in this case, happened to be a softball toss into silver milk jugs.

"Do we, now?" I said, handing over my money in exchange for three big balls.

Quentin leaned on the counter to watch.

Focusing on the first jug, I lightly lobbed the ball. It circled around the spout before falling inside.

Quentin let out a low whistle.

The second ball dropped almost directly inside the second jug, and by the time I'd moved down to the third, he was staring at me like I was some kind of alien life-form.

When the third ball made it in, I dusted off my hands and glanced over at him. "Well, *most* girls can't win their own."

He shook his head. "Seriously impressed."

I laughed at the note of reverence in his voice. When the guy handed me a stuffed unicorn that was practically the same size as me, I held it toward Quentin. "For you."

He was still shaking his head. "Who *are* you?"

I shrugged and smiled.

"How did you do that?" he asked, wrangling the unicorn around his shoulders like he was giving it a piggyback ride.

"I know people who know things. All kinds of people and all kinds of things." When he rolled his hand, waiting, I added, "When we were in Munich one time, I met some boy whose family owned a big traveling carnival. He taught me a few tricks to the games that he probably shouldn't have."

Quentin took the last bite of his cheesecake and tossed the skewer into the closest garbage can. "And why ever would this boy want to give you his family business's most valued secrets?" From his tone alone, I knew exactly what he was getting at.

I elbowed him in the ribs. "Because I was nice to him and he was a nice person."

"A nice person who was hoping you'd exchange 'nice' favors for his trade secrets."

Another elbow. "No, he wasn't."

Quentin stared over at me with a little smile on his face. "You're kinda adorable when you're naive."

I ignored the jab and checked my phone again. It was close to eleven, and I wasn't sure how long I should stay out. The later I was out, the worse it would be if I got caught, I guessed. With Mom, I hadn't hesitated to be gone all night. But this was my first time under Aunt Julie's watch, *and* I was with a boy. A boy I liked, despite knowing I probably shouldn't. It felt different being out late with a guy I liked, more serious.

"Rides," Quentin said, pointing to the next thing. He wasn't ready for the night to be over. I wasn't, either. Stopping in front of the ticket booth, he freed his wallet again. A reminder chimed in my head.

"Here's your change." I retrieved his money left over from the other day and handed it to him. "I would have gotten it to you a while ago, but family emergencies and Mr. Snuggles searches kept getting in the way."

"Yeah, sorry about that." Quentin added the money to what he already had in his hand and gave it to the cashier. "I promised to cover you during a break, so now I owe you two breaks next time we work together."

"You don't owe me anything."

"But I told you I would." He somehow managed to keep the giant unicorn balanced on his shoulders with one hand while he pocketed his wallet. "I do what I say I'm going to do, and I take care of my responsibilities."

My head tipped as he took the tickets and started toward the rides. "But I'm not your responsibility."

He cleared his throat, moving into the back of the Ferris wheel line. "But maybe I want to take care of you."

"Why?"

"Because I like you."

I shifted. "In what way?"

It was our turn to step up and hand off our tickets. After the operator motioned us toward the car, Quentin glanced over at me. "You know what way."

He didn't say anything else as he rolled the unicorn off his shoulders to get it situated. I did my best not to look surprised or thrown, but I felt it. Big-time. One moment Quentin seemed like the type of guy who kept everything to himself, and the next he was looking me in the eye and admitting he liked me.

I got in, clutching my small bear, and Quentin climbed in after me, putting the unicorn on the end so we were next to each other. Like, *right* beside one another. As in, his leg running down the side of mine, his shoulder and arm sandwiched against mine.

After the Ferris wheel operator made sure we were locked in, the wheel started to move to the next couple.

"Sorry if I made things weird saying that," Quentin started. "I know I'm supposed to play it cool or whatever, but you seem like the kind of person who would appreciate the up-front and honest approach."

I was that kind of person. Except maybe not in this instance, because I wasn't ready to be up-front and honest about how I felt about him yet. Since I didn't know what to say, I didn't say anything. Thankfully he played along and didn't push the issue.

The Ferris wheel started to circle around, distracting us both as we took in the sights. I couldn't decide which was more fun to look at—the dark ocean or the bright lights glowing beneath us. I'd ridden lots of Ferris wheels, all different kinds, but this one was my favorite yet.

That might have had to do with the way Quentin's hand had just slipped into mine, his fingers braiding through mine one at a time. He didn't say anything; he simply took my hand. I didn't say anything, either; I just held his hand, too.

A few more turns later the wheel came to a stop; the slow process of unloading and reloading passengers began. I wasn't sure if fate was responsible or if Quentin had tipped the ride operator, but it couldn't have been a random coincidence that we were stuck up at the very top.

His hand pressed a little deeper into mine as I noticed him angle his body toward me. He didn't say anything.

From the corner of my eye, I noticed his mouth start to slide into a crooked smile, like he was reading my thoughts. "You can kiss me, you know, if you want to. Just putting that out there."

My mouth fell open a little. "I don't want to kiss you. Who do you think I am?" I did my best to sound insulted, but I felt more panicked than anything.

His head moved. "Some girl who wants to kiss me?"

"Um, no. Got that wrong." I tried to scoot away, but because of the ridiculous unicorn, I mostly ended up rubbing against his leg.

He scooted along with me. "Really?"

"Yeah, really." I shook my hand out of his. "Why? Do you want to kiss me?"

"Well, I did," he said, motioning at me, "until you started acting like you'd rather make out with a pissed-off porcupine."

The Ferris wheel suddenly lowered us down a notch. We were still up high, but we weren't at the tippy-top.

"You seriously missed out on a great first kiss." Quentin's eyes drifted above to where we'd been. "One straight from the pages of one of those romance books you like so much. But I guess I was right about you wanting to read about life instead of live it."

My arms folded over my body. "I read classics, by the way, not romances."

He snorted. "Same thing."

If there was a way to throw myself out of this thing without the side effect of death, I would have been gone. "No, classics are tragic, darker, more realistic than all of that over-the-top happy-ending BS."

He gave me a funny look. "You don't like happy endings?"

"I like realistic endings. They're more relatable," I answered, cooling myself down. A little. "They don't set some impossible bar or an unattainable standard."

"You're not secretly looking for your Prince Charming?" he asked in a mock-serious voice, which made me smile. From swooning to outraged to amused. All in one Ferris wheel ride.

"If I was, what would I be doing here with you?"

That made him laugh as we lowered down another spot. "Well, you aren't exactly the princess type, either."

"That's the nicest thing you've ever said to me."

He rubbed at the back of his head. "You're full of surprises, you know that, Jade Abbott?"

"I do know that. Glad you figured that out."

"Yeah?"

I leaned in, like I was about to let him in on a secret. "So when you discover I'm really an undercover agent trying to find the kingpin responsible for laundering money from the concession stand at the public pool, you won't bat an eye."

"Not one eye will bat, I swear," he laughed, his expression taking on a serious tone. "You know, I'm full of surprises, too."

That was one of the most obvious statements I'd heard. "Yeah, I know you are."

When his hand found mine again, I left it there for the rest of the ride and the rest of the night. By the time he dropped me back at my place a little after midnight, my hand felt strange not having his around it. Almost like a part of him had already become a part of me.

Chapter Ten

Operation Sneaking Out was a success. My aunt was none the wiser, and I'd made it back home in one whole, unscathed piece. It wasn't a proud moment—going behind her back—but it was an important one. I wasn't going to spend the summer locked in a pink bedroom or stuffed inside a suffocating concession stand.

My job at the pool had become easier lately, but things with Quentin were more difficult. Keeping up with a long line of customers and trying to do five things at once was simple compared to whatever was going on between us. Our shifts usually overlapped an hour or two, but when he was at work, he was at work. In the zone and focused. When he took his breaks or covered for me so I could take mine, he morphed into the Quentin I'd gotten a glimpse of that night at the carnival. The carefree, fun Quentin whose smile could turn my insides to mush.

It was one of those overcast days that was struggling to hit seventy, which meant the pool was quiet. A few kids were chattering in the water while their moms were scattered around the perimeter bundled up in leggings and UGGs.

The concession stand was the least busy I'd ever seen, which gave me loads of free time to waste on my phone. Quentin wasn't working until two, when my shift ended, but I was hoping to work a "surreptitious" run-in to say hi or something.

After our night at the carnival, I'd kind of expected him to follow up or swing by or, I don't know, call, but he hadn't. He waved across the pool at me a couple of times and he smiled when one of us showed up for a shift while the other was leaving, but that was it.

How could a guy drop an "I like you" bomb on a girl and then carry on for a whole week like nothing had happened? Was he waiting for me to call the next shot? Allowing me time to take the lead? Had he changed his mind? Did he have an identical twin I'd gone out with last week?

To distract myself, I pulled up my dad's social media profile again, checking for any recent posts I might have missed. He posted more than kids my age did, everything from PSAs that were totally condescending to photos of him with his "bros" at whatever bar they'd just played or stumbled into.

Since yesterday afternoon, he'd already added six more posts, including a photo of him with some girl who'd been at his show last night and asked for his autograph. On her chest.

It was a really weird feeling, like I should be similar to this person, since he was my father, only I didn't have one thing in common with him other than maybe my wide-set eyes.

Ignoring the pit that opened up in my stomach when I

thought about confronting my dad, I moved on to punching in a text to Mom. It was way wordy by the time I hit send.

I missed her. And I knew she missed me, which made it that much worse. As much as I was settling into life here and enjoying getting to see the same scenery for more than a week at a time, part of me missed that life, too. Not enough to abort my summer plans and catch the first flight to wherever the Shrinking Violets were playing next, but enough to make my throat get all tight when I thought about it.

"So I'm going to put this out there, since I've made a habit of that when it comes to you." I jumped, dropping my phone when Quentin seemed to appear out of nowhere. "I've been waiting for you to decide what comes next. I've been pretty obvious about how I feel, but you've been pretty *unobvious* about it all." He leaned across the counter, putting as little space between us as he could. "Do you like me or not?"

I gave myself a moment before answering. "In what way are you defining *like* in this instance?"

"At this point, I'll be happy with any form of like. Even if it's just you liking me when I walk away." He was in a bulky navy sweatshirt today, with big white letters spelling *LIFE-GUARD* across the front. The whites of his eyes were a little red, and the hollows beneath were dark. Looked like more sleepless nights.

"Okay, well then, yeah, I like you." I stuffed my phone into the back pocket of my jeans.

"Like me how, exactly?" Half of his face pulled up.

I sighed. "I like you when you walk away."

I didn't expect him to actually start walking away.

"Quentin." He stopped the moment I started saying his

name. "Can we just let this unfold on its own? See where it goes instead of trying to put a name to it right this very moment?" My heart felt like it was about to burst from my chest, that's how hard it was beating from having him close and talking to me after a week of silence.

He looked at me. "You're calling the shots here."

A streak of boldness hit me—it might have had something to do with the way I'd spent the past week of my summer either working or hanging with my aunt when I was supposed to be living it up.

"Got any plans tonight?"

His eyes flashed at me. "Maybe. But I could be persuaded into something else."

"Nine-thirty tonight. I'll meet you in front of your place."

His smile formed. I was pretty much infatuated with it by now. "What's the plan?"

I lifted a shoulder. "The not knowing's half the fun."

Night number two of sneaking from my aunt and uncle's house had just been added to the tally. Uncle Paul was out of town for work, and Aunt Julie hadn't thought anything about a seventeen-year-old going to bed at nine o'clock on a summer Friday night. I knew that was because she trusted me, which made me feel that much more guilty about sneaking out.

I'd considered telling her I had plans to go hang with a friend tonight, only to realize the list of questions that would inevitably follow. She wouldn't say yes to me leaving late at night with a boy, no matter how "nice" she thought Quentin seemed. I guessed it had something to do with what had happened to my mom when she went off alone with a boy as a teenager.

Like last week, Quentin came out of his front door, this time calling a few good-byes inside before closing it behind him. Clearly his parents didn't have any issues with him leaving late-ish at night with a girl. Their family didn't have a sore spot like Aunt Julie did for what "could" happen when a boy and girl went off alone.

"Prompt," I greeted as he loped closer, his smile in the on position. He had no idea what I had planned for the night.

"No way I'd show up late for a date you asked me out on."

Something fluttered in my stomach when he stopped in front of me. "This isn't a date."

"Then what is it?" he asked, waiting as I worked on how to answer that. When I struggled to find the right term, his smile crept higher. "This is *so* a date."

I moved to slug him, but he caught my hand, his fingers winding around my wrist. "But you can go ahead and call it whatever you want and I'll play along."

My mouth parted, thanks to the way my breath started to speed up. That was when I noticed something in the big window facing into the yard. When I glanced in that direction, I saw a woman standing there, frowning at us with concern. She was tall and pretty, and I could see where Quentin had gotten plenty of his good looks from.

"By the way, thank you for the gift you left me on my doorstep a few days ago." He nudged me. "And the sweet note along with it."

I had to work really hard to keep a straight face. Dragging

that huge-ass box of books back to his place had not been easy. But so very worth it.

"I keep the note on my nightstand, so I can fall asleep to your words every night." Quentin's hand tightened a little around my wrist. *"You need these more than I do,"* he said, reciting the very note I'd left him when I returned his special "gift." *"Since romance is obviously a foreign concept to you."*

"Have you been studying up?" I asked. "Plenty of good material in that giant box."

He leaned in, his eyes staying on mine the whole time. "You'll have to be the judge of that."

When I shifted, clearing my throat, his expression started to move into a gloat. "Come on. I can't be gone as late tonight," he said, letting go of my wrist and starting for his truck.

"Curfew?" I guessed, having heard of them but never having any personal experience with one.

His head shook. "Responsibilities."

I nodded, remembering seeing his name on the schedule for the early shift tomorrow. "Hey, where do you think you're going?"

He had the passenger door of his truck open for me. "Waiting for you to get in the truck and give me directions."

When I rolled around the bikes I'd leaned up against his tailgate, he gaped at them like they were alien objects. "And I'm waiting for you to climb onto one of these and follow me."

"You're not serious, right?" He motioned between his truck and the bikes like I wasn't making sense.

I held my ground.

"Okay, remind me why we're riding bikes when I've got a

perfectly good truck with a full tank of gas?" he said, closing the door and trudging toward the bikes. After getting Lemon fixed up, I'd found another one in half-decent condition shoved into Uncle Paul's storage shed.

"Because the best way to see a city is either on foot or on a bike."

"And the best way to get from point A to point B is three hundred horsepower," he jested. "Plus, it's my city—I know there's nothing here to explore."

Sighing, I motioned to the helmet hanging off the handlebars. "Get on already."

Quentin frowned as he shoved the helmet onto his head. "Only because you asked so nicely."

I had to turn my head to keep from laughing at the way he was pouting. Once he threw his leg over the bike, I swung mine over Lemon and started down the sidewalk, making sure he was following.

He was. With the least enthusiastic look I'd ever seen— faking it all the way.

"Now I see why you'd want to try a summer somewhere else if this is how you've been spending your time." Quentin pedaled up beside me, looking like he was in pain.

"I don't know. I'm starting to question why I glorified the normal American teenage life. The most exciting thing I've done the past week is make chalk flowers on the sidewalk with my little cousins."

"Please tell me you're not being serious right now."

"Why do you have such a difficult time believing me?" I asked, swerving onto the street when the sidewalk came to an end. Quentin followed right behind me.

"Because it's seriously pathetic if that's the most exciting thing you've done all week."

"Yeah? So what's the coolest thing you've done this week?" I asked.

"We're talking about you here, not me. I've lived up plenty of summers already."

"Sure, you have." I didn't dull the sarcasm.

"You're only young once. Don't waste it being old." He came around me so I was closer to the curb than he was.

"Says the teenager talking about responsibilities and priorities in life."

He pretended not to hear me, instead speeding ahead so I had to chase him down. It was kind of nice riding with someone. Usually I cruised around on my own; sometimes Mom would join me if she wasn't performing, but it was fun to share all of the sights and sounds I was experiencing with someone new.

It wasn't long before we turned down a couple of busy streets, but we weren't far from home. Quentin stayed beside me in the bike lane, no longer complaining about our mode of transportation. Actually, he was enjoying himself.

The restaurant was right up ahead, and as I slowed I hoped he might not notice the name.

"The Veg Head? For real?" No such luck. Quentin crawled off his bike beside me, staring into the restaurant like he was expecting to find an actual train wreck or something. "First a bike and now this? Are you trying to turn me into some kind of hippie, woman?"

After securing our bikes to the racks outside, I headed for the front door. He beat me to it, holding it open. "You got to decide on our first outing, it's only fair I get to call the shots on this one," I fired at him.

"What? So we have some kind of unsaid agreement now? I plan a date, you plan a date?"

I stalled inside the door. "This isn't a date. This is a non-date."

"Well, if this is a nondate, there should definitely be some veto power built into this arrangement. You know, so one of us isn't forced to choke down—"

"Healthy food?" I said as we moved through the restaurant. I picked one of the window tables toward the back so the pizza place across the street wouldn't tempt him.

"Of all the places you could have taken me, of all the things we could have done . . ." Quentin paused beside the table, doing a slow spin as he gaped at the restaurant. He took a seat across from me. "Really?"

"I was hungry, and not for fried heart disease on a stick, thank you very much," I argued, before he had a chance to make another dining suggestion. "And I thought this would be a nice way to just, you know, talk." I lifted my menu to distract myself from him.

"*Vegan tofu nachos?*" The look on his face as he read the menu almost made me laugh. "So much wrongness right there. I can't even . . ."

"You should try the grilled tofu steak with mango sauce. I heard that's good."

Quentin's eyes went wider the farther down he made it on the menu. "First of all, the word *steak* should never, *ever* be next to the word *tofu. Ever.*" When I started to open my mouth, he continued, "Second, who did you hear it was good from? Besides nobody in the history of ever." He leaned across the table and whispered like it was a secret. "Tofu."

"Fine. We can go somewhere else if you're going to act like a baby." I was already standing up when Quentin's hand curled around mine.

"We're here." His shoulders lifted in a what-the-hell kind of way. "One healthy meal won't kill me."

He kept holding my hand, which seemed to directly affect the steadiness in my knees. "No. But it might kill *me* if you keep whining."

His eyes twinkled. "Tempting offer."

The waitress appeared, but it took me a moment to regain my senses.

"I'll have the grilled tofu *steak* with mango sauce," Quentin ordered when I stayed quiet. "I hear it's 'good.'"

It wasn't until he finally let go of my hand that I was able to articulate. "And I'll have the namaste roll and the asparagus gazpacho."

The server filled our water glasses before leaving. I'd downed half of mine by the time she disappeared into the kitchen.

"So this is the type of place you like? The kind you visit when you're traveling the world?" His face gave nothing away, but his tone did. His voice suggested that I was unhinged if this was what I sought out when the planet was my playground.

"A girl's gotta eat," I answered. "And it isn't exactly easy trying to cook meals with hot plates and hotel microwaves.

But trying to find a place like this in Argentina, the country where they consider beef to be a God-given right, is pretty much impossible. They just felt sorry for me whenever I tried explaining that I didn't eat meat."

Quentin spun his glass of water around in slow circles as he listened to me. "What's it like?"

"What's what like?"

"Traveling? Seeing the world?"

"Oh, it's nice, I guess. It's the only life I've ever known. That was the whole reason for this summer. So I could see . . . something else. Something everyone else gets to experience."

Quentin huffed, shaking his head. "Trust me, globe-trotting is far more exciting than any American teenager's life."

I tucked my leg beneath me. "Maybe. What about you? What's your life like?"

When he was quiet for a minute, I started to wonder if my question was somehow inappropriate.

"It's nice," he said to his water glass with a yawn. He looked like he would have benefited from another one of those power naps in his truck. "Complicated but good."

"Complicated how?" I knew *complicated* was a loaded word, an all-encompassing explanation for everything from being late to class to fights with BFFs.

Quentin answered my question by tapping a pinkie on his glass, keeping his mouth shut.

It was one of the only times he seemed to prefer staying quiet over nonstop rambling. "My aunt told me your family moved in recently. Where did you guys move from?" I thought this question could break the ice so he'd be more willing to answer more of them.

"Just a couple hours north is all. Not far." He took a drink of water, draining nearly the entire glass.

"Did that suck, having to move to a new school your junior year?"

He shook his head. "No, it was actually kind of nice. A fresh start, you know?" When he looked at me, it was like he was waiting for me to back him up, but my experience led me to another conclusion.

"I've had seventeen years of fresh starts. Every few days or weeks. For once, it would be nice to hang around long enough to really get to know people, and for them to get to know me."

Quentin was grinning, like he was in on some secret I wasn't. "Trust me. Staying isn't all it's cracked up to be."

"But neither is traveling everywhere and belonging nowhere."

As the server returned with our orders, Quentin scooted his sleeves up his arms, like he had to psych himself up to tear into his tofu steak. "Yeah, well, I guess I'll have to take your word for it."

"You're seventeen, you know?" I said after thanking the server when she slid my order in front of me. "You can figure it out on your own soon."

"Nah, I'll have to do the whole living-vicariously-through-you thing." He was staring at his plate, unsure.

"You're graduating from high school in a year."

"Yep, and three months later I'm off to college."

After placing my napkin on my lap, I picked up my spoon. "They have those all over the world. There's even programs where you can study abroad."

When Quentin stabbed at his grilled tofu with his fork, he winced. "There's also this community college a half-hour drive from my house."

My spoon froze in my gazpacho. "You're staying here?"

"Yep." He lifted his first bite to his mouth.

"Why?"

"It's cheap." He ate the tofu. Then he finished the rest of his water.

"It's cheap? That's your reason for picking community college? There are scholarships. You could still travel all over."

He scooted his empty glass to the end of the table. "I want to stay close to my family. They need me, you know? They depend on me. I couldn't just bounce on them like that."

Had I just come face to face with the most responsible teenage boy ever? "Pretty sure your family would be support-ive of your dreams."

His head tipped. "That's *one* of my reasons."

"What are the others?"

"*My* reasons."

If his voice didn't say it, his eyes did when they met mine. *Leave it alone.*

I tried the soup so I wouldn't be tempted to ask dozens of follow-up questions.

"So your mom's in a band." Quentin gave me a questioning look, his spoon aimed at my soup. When I nodded, he dipped his spoon into my soup hesitantly. "What does your dad do?"

The roll I was picking up slipped from my hands. "Uh, he's in a band, too."

"Really?" Quentin said, tasting my soup. He didn't even grimace. At least not too badly.

"Really."

"Wow, so how do they work around each other's tour schedules?"

"Um, well, they aren't together or anything." I tried mirroring his *Leave it alone* look, but it didn't work.

"When did they get divorced?"

"No divorce." I cleared my throat and took a sip of water before scooting my glass down beside his. Water emergency at table nine. "They were never married."

He was quiet for a moment. "Do you guys ever see him?"

I stalled with some more soup. "My mom hasn't seen him since she was my age, right after she told him she was pregnant."

"And, what? He just bailed?"

The word sounded harsh, but it was what had happened. "Pretty much."

Quentin snorted across from me. "So you've never even met your real dad?"

No. Nope. I haven't. I have not. I shook my head.

He ground his jaw as his hands curled into fists. I hadn't expected this kind of response from him. At all. It was almost like it was as personal to him as it was to me.

I worked on the namaste roll I wasn't really tasting, in uncomfortable silence.

"I'm sorry, Jade. That's a shit thing to do to someone."

"Well, in his defense, he hadn't met me before he ditched.

Because I'm sure if he had, I totally would have changed his mind. I'm just that awesome." I beamed at him like I believed it, and it seemed to work. He was back to acting chill and like nothing in the world could get to him.

"You *are* awesome. I'm sure if he did have a chance to get to know you, he wouldn't go anywhere."

I set my roll down and wondered if he was right. I'd find out soon enough.

"Do you feel like, I don't know, something big's missing from your life?" Quentin was staring at the table, his forehead creased.

I wanted conversation and getting to know each other— I was getting it.

After the server came around with the water pitcher, we both reached for our refilled glasses at the same time. "I've never met my dad. Ever. So yeah, I feel like something's missing."

His eyes met mine. "Missing how?"

I had thought about that question probably longer than any other in my life. I gave him the only answer I'd ever come up with: "I don't know."

Chapter Eleven

I never thought I'd wake up to a sunny morning and actually whine about it, but that was a side effect of working at a public pool concession stand in the middle of the summer.

I was working way more than I'd planned, but that was okay since the alternative was hanging with Aunt Julie and the twins. She'd loosened the collar . . . if I considered going to the grocery store alone a win. Other than the occasional night Quentin and I schemed to sneak out for some random adventure, that was about as exciting as my summer had been.

But I was fast becoming a pro at not getting caught sneaking out—the true American teen way. Mom would have been so proud. If she'd known. Which I wasn't about to tell her on the off chance she accidently mentioned it to Aunt Julie when they checked in with each other every few days.

"Switch you." Zoey scooted up next to the freezer, where I hadn't stopped scooping ice cream in what felt like eons.

"You're my hero," I sighed, gladly handing her the scoop as I took her place behind the cash register. It was rare that

I had help during a shift, but the week of Fourth of July was especially busy, so Janet had us all working extra shifts.

"Hey, a bunch of us are going to go chill on my stepdad's boat tonight if you want to come. We won't actually be leaving the dock or anything, but it will be fun regardless." Zoey dropped her scoop into the vanilla ice cream tub when she heard the kid's order as he unloaded a fistful of quarters onto the counter.

"Will your friend be there?" My gaze automatically drifted to the lounger where one of Zoey's friends was stretched out, adjusting her string top for the hundredth time. Instead of adjusting it so more of herself was covered, she was adjusting it so less was covered. I couldn't miss the way she stared over in Quentin's direction as she did. Luckily, he was in super-lifeguard mode and therefore oblivious to the whole thing.

"She's not really my friend. More friend-of-a-friend type of thing. I'm sorry again about earlier, though. I don't know what Ashlyn's problem was." Zoey shot me another apologetic smile before stacking three scoops of ice cream onto a cone.

From what had been going on before she came sashaying up to the concession stand, I guessed I had an idea as to what her problem was: Quentin. Well, I guessed her problem was me, and how Quentin's attention had been on me earlier when she'd practically stumbled chest-first into him when she ordered her Diet Coke.

"Don't worry about it. I wouldn't know what to do if someone didn't try putting me in my place weekly. It might mess with my sense of self-worth. Totally give me a positive self-image or something dangerous like that." I counted out how many quarters the kid owed me, then scooted the rest back toward him.

Zoey was shaking her head, laughing a little as she braced herself for the next order. Her shoulders sagged in relief when the kid ordered a hot dog meal. "I can't believe you actually just smiled after that, handed over her change, and said, 'Have a nice day.'" Zoey laughed again. "I mean, come on, who does that?"

"What else was I supposed to say?" I slid my braid behind my back, trying not to stare at Quentin as he rotated to his next post. Trying not to stare, like all the other girls around my age. I was about as successful as the rest of them, too.

"Um, I don't know, take your pick of bitchy responses. There's literally no shortage of them." Even Zoey was watching Quentin. It was kind of hard not to. Especially with the way he was smiling at a few kids who had just gotten to the pool and were waving at him like he was the greatest thing since summer vacation.

"Nah, it's okay. And besides, she was kind of right. I am kind of a hippie, and right now I am pretty dirty." I held out my arms, which were streaked with smears of ice cream. Shoot, even my shoes had splatters of nacho cheese on them from earlier. "But I'm not a skank. Whatever a skank is, because I'm not sure if that's been accurately defined."

Zoey squeezed a glob of ketchup on the dog and wrapped it up. "As a friend of a friend, I'm apologizing for her, but yeah, she probably will be there tonight, so I totally get if you want to take a pass."

My shoulders raised as I made change. Working the

register was so much better than prepping the food. "Actually, it isn't really her, but it's more my aunt. She wouldn't let me come anyway. But thanks for the invite."

"Why not?" Zoey blew a wisp of hair from her eyes as she handed me the hot dog meal.

"Because she's worried I'll get into trouble or something."

"Please." Zoey exhaled sharply. "You are, like, the most responsible human being I've ever met. What's she so worried about?"

"That I'll get knocked up, the dad will run away, and I will ruin my and my baby's life thanks to one bad decision."

When Zoey blinked at me, I remembered that sometimes honesty was best served lukewarm.

"Anyway, thanks again for the invite. Maybe some other time."

Zoey smiled and got to work on the next order. I'd just turned down a party on a boat with a bunch of people my age on the Fourth of July. Yeah, so maybe it was a docked boat, and maybe one of those people my age had called me a dirty skank hippie, but really? This was why I'd come here this summer. These kinds of experiences. I wanted to listen to my aunt, and I wasn't the rebel type, but I was about to become one if things didn't change soon.

I was in the zone, taking and filling orders in record time, when I noticed someone press himself up against my side of the counter. Press his nice, firm-looking tan chest up against the counter.

"What are you doing tonight?" Quentin asked abruptly, like we'd already exchanged heys and how-are-you-doings.

When I took a minute to answer, Zoey nudged me. "I

invited her out on my stepdad's boat, but she said her aunt wouldn't let her."

Quentin started to smirk at me. "Look at you. Living it up." He tapped at his watch face, like the second hand was a day hand, and they were ticking away.

"I've had a perfectly great summer so far." My voice was more than a little defensive, but he was poking at a sore subject.

"So? Perfectly great summer?" His smirk deepened. "What have you got planned for tonight?"

He had me. He *knew* he had me.

Because I didn't have anything planned for tonight, one of the most celebrated holidays in the whole entire nation. One particularly popular with those my age because it was synonymous with summer and swimsuits, I guessed.

"Barbecue at my place. Seven o'clock." It wasn't a question, but he cocked his head and waited.

Beside me, I noticed Zoey's mouth start to open.

He must have guessed where my mind had led me because he added, "My mom said your family's invited, so bring everyone. We used to do a big get-together every Fourth back before we moved. This will be our first one here in the new place, so there won't be as many people, but it will still be cool."

Zoey scooted closer, like she was hoping proximity might earn her an invitation, too.

"Oh, and I told my mom you're one of those masochists who doesn't eat meat or cheese or any food that's delicious, so we've got you covered."

Something squeezed in my chest, and I didn't stop to think about my answer before giving in. "See you at seven."

Quentin tapped the counter, smiling at me before leaving.

Beside me still, Zoey elbowed me. "Did Quentin Ford ask you on a date?"

I wondered what she'd say if she knew about our late-night get-togethers-slash-hangouts-slash-dates.

"He only asked my family over to his house for dinner." I got back to taking orders, not missing the lethal expression Zoey's friend of a friend was firing my way. She didn't even know what he'd said, and she was looking at me like she wanted to squash me with her platform sandals.

"He asked *you* over to *his* place. That's what that was, you know, in case you needed a translation."

Instead of arguing with her about what that was or wasn't, I asked, "Do you know Quentin? You know, outside of the pool?"

Zoey snagged a bag of chips from the rack and tossed them at the girl who'd ordered them. "He transferred to my school last year, but I don't really *know* him. Although I wouldn't mind knowing him, the way I'm guessing he's hoping to know you." Zoey winked over at me.

"What's he like at school?"

"Exactly like he is here. Friendly, works hard, keeps to himself mostly."

My forehead creased. "He keeps to himself?"

"Well, yeah, pretty much. Other than a wicked smile here, a flirty wink there, yeah, he's kinda a loner. The hottest loner ever, but still."

"Really?" My head tipped as I watched him. He didn't seem like the keep-to-himself loner type at all. Even though

I'd never really seen him with anyone outside of work . . . besides me.

"I think he and his family are really close. The type that does all kinds of things together. Plus, with him being the oldest, you know his parents force him into babysitting duty all of the time." Zoey handed off a lopsided chocolate cone to a kid who was barely as tall as that ice cream was.

"So what are you going to wear?" Zoey asked, like this was the question to end all questions.

I held out my arms and did a spin. Crochet top and cut-offs. Perfect.

"That is not what one wears to the house of the Quentin Fords of the world," Zoey said, all solemn-like.

My eyes lifted as I took the next order. "I'm not changing for anyone. Not even Quentin Ford."

Okay, so maybe I changed for Quentin Ford. But only my outfit, and only because before my shift ended, I'd managed to pour nacho cheese down my shirt instead of on the tray of chips I was serving.

I was trying to distract myself from the fact that I was heading up Quentin's walkway with my aunt and little cousins. Even though it was the Fourth, Uncle Paul had to go in to work, but he'd promised to make it back in time for fireworks. I wasn't holding my breath, and from the look on his eight-year-olds' faces, neither were they.

"Are you sure I shouldn't have picked up flowers, too? I don't feel right showing up for a dinner party without flowers for the hostess." Aunt Julie was fretting her lower lip as we walked up the porch, looking like she was about to be accused of high treason.

"Aunt Julie, it's fine. I texted Quentin to ask his mom what we could bring and all she said was just ourselves." I stopped at the front door, glancing over at the canvas shopping bags my aunt had filled to the brim with goodies to share. "And you're here with wine, sparkling cider, festive cupcakes, and whatever else you stuffed into those bags." Pretty sure I caught a peek of a fruit salad nestled beneath the cupcakes. "And it's a barbecue. Not a dinner party."

The twins were in matching patriotic rompers and had their hair French-braided so tightly it looked like it was pulling their eyebrows up. They seemed excited, like they were hoping they'd get to run around and work on a few grass stains instead of running a bow across a violin or counting in Chinese.

"Now, girls—"

Before she could list off the hundred rules that came with every outing, Hailey piped up, "Be on your best behavior, be respectful, and be kind."

Aunt Julie nodded, looking a little nervous, like she shouldn't have let me talk her into this a whole three hours ago. Just in case she was thinking about running, I rang the doorbell.

It sounded like a herd of bison was rushing the door, right before a crashing pounded against it.

Aunt Julie gave me a look, like I'd led her and the twins into a trap, and then a kid opened the door. He looked a couple years older than the twins; his younger brother elbowed his way into the doorway, too. For such small humans, they sure made a lot of noise.

"Which one of you is Quentin's girlfriend?" one of them asked, crossing his arms and glaring with accusation at Aunt Julie and the twins.

When Aunt Julie's head snapped my way, I smiled all reassuring-like. "I'm Quentin's friend, who's a girl. We work together at the pool."

He sized me up, right before the door opened the rest of the way and Quentin's mom stepped forward. "Hello, so nice to finally have you and the girls over, Julie," Mrs. Ford said, although I didn't miss the way Mrs. Ford looked at me . . . dangerous. "And you must be Jade. This is Silas"—Mrs. Ford rubbed the older boy's head—"and this is Abe." The younger one stood up taller and checked out the twins, deciding whether they had cooties. The verdict: yes.

Mrs. Ford must have noticed me glancing around, because she waved toward the sliding door in the kitchen—"Quentin's out back"—before turning to Aunt Julie.

Quentin's out back. No Hi, I'm Mrs. Ford. Welcome. Or What's your name? It was obvious Mrs. Ford wasn't a fan, but how could she not like me when she didn't even know me yet?

Maybe I really did give off a dirty skank hippie vibe.

As I wandered through the house, I noticed how different it was from Aunt Julie's tidy, bordering-on-compulsively-clean house. Don't get me wrong, it wasn't filthy or anything like that, but stuff was out of place. Furniture appeared used instead of on display. Toys were scattered around counters and floors. Dishes sat in the sink. It was a house that was lived in.

When I swung through the sliding glass door, the first thing I noticed was Quentin's dad hovering over one of those big bright baby bouncers. He was tickling and making faces at the baby girl inside, and she was eating it up. Her chubby little thighs jiggled as she bounced up and down, giggling so hard that she was making spit bubbles.

His dad was clearly preoccupied, so I wandered over to where Quentin was hovering in front of a grill, his back toward me.

"Look at you, Chef Boyardee." I smiled as I moved up behind him, noticing the way he was holding his tongs like he was ready to fight a medieval war with them at any moment.

When Quentin peeked over at me, his eyes widened at the same time his breath seemed to get stuck in his throat. "Look at you," he said, waving his tongs as he inspected me in a way that made my own breath fail to cooperate. When his gaze ended on where the hem of my dress was floating above my knee, one side of his mouth lifted. "You didn't have to go and get all dressed up on my account."

I crossed my arms. "I didn't. It's the nation's holiday. I got dressed up for America's birthday."

"Sure, convenient. I'm wearing a pretty dress because the United States is turning two hundred and fortyish years old. FYI, Jade, America's blind as a bat. It can't see what you're wearing or not wearing to its birthday." When he said *not wearing,* he wiggled his brows a few times.

My arms crossed tighter, but this time it was to keep my stomach from coming unraveled from the way he was studying me. "You don't seem to be having a difficult time looking."

He shook his head slowly. "Fifty states. Three point eight million square miles. Twenty thousand cities. Three hundred and twenty million people. That's a lot of looking to make up for."

Okay, so yeah. I was kind of thrilled I'd changed for Quentin Ford, even if it was something as minor as wardrobe.

"What are you working on there?" I checked the barbecue to distract myself—and hopefully him. He wasn't as easily distracted as I was.

"Portobello mushrooms. I marinated them and everything." Pinching his tongs a few times, he started to turn them over, distracted.

"You made these?"

"Yeah." I must have been giving him a shocked look because he sighed. "They're big mushrooms, Jade, not nuclear physics."

His dad was now stationed in front of the other giant grill built into the big deck, flipping over what looked like burgers and hot dogs.

"Why aren't you grilling them over there on that thing? It looks big enough to fit a thousand mushrooms."

When Quentin shrugged, I noticed the way his shirt tugged across his shoulders, like it wasn't quite large enough to fit him.

"I didn't want them to, you know, come in contact with any of that devil food known as meat over there." His eyes flashed at me. "No meat by-product on your pure vegetables."

125

My arms uncrossed. "You're kind of thoughtful when you put your mind to it, you know that?" I nudged him, saying it like it was a secret.

"Not thoughtful, just self-serving," he whispered, playing along.

"How is you making me mushroom burgers on a separate grill self-serving?"

He stepped out of arm's reach, which meant he was about to say something that would earn him a swat or a slug. "Because by doing so, I'm banking on you letting me round second base later tonight."

I was stunned, but before I could fire off any comeback, he clapped his tongs at a heap of stuff stacked up close by. Baseball mitts, bats, balls, and a few plastic plates lying at the ready.

"We're on separate teams; we already drew straws earlier." Quentin was gloating by now, loving that he'd totally pulled one over on me. "I make you dinner, you let me slide into third."

My hand settled onto my hip. "You can have third. I'll be the one sliding into home."

He leaned in closer, until I could smell the faint scent of soap clinging to his skin. His green eyes were shining down at me. "Lucky for me I play catcher."

My expression gave the impression he was annoying me, but that wasn't quite right. Flustered was more what I felt, especially with the way he was looking at me. A sharp cry roused me from my temporary hypnosis.

Quentin's gaze immediately moved from me to where the baby was. "Baby or barbecue?" he asked, already handing over the tongs like he knew my answer.

I knew more about babies than I did barbecues. There's no way Mom or I could be trusted around an open flame.

"Baby," I said immediately, backing away from the tongs.

"Really?" Quentin said. "Most teens I know are more scared of babies than they are of becoming a social outcast."

I walked over to the bouncer. "I'm already a social outcast," I said.

Crouching down so we were mostly at eye level, I held out my arms to see how she felt about me picking her up. She wasn't crying anymore, but she was blinking up at me like she wasn't sure what to think.

She gave that a moment's thought, examining my face like she was reading some kind of ingredient label pasted to my forehead. Then she bounced around a couple of times and cracked a smile as she held out her pudgy little arms toward me.

"I like you, too," I said, hoisting her from the bouncer carefully. Quentin's dad had disappeared inside, so I wandered back toward Quentin and the mushrooms. He wasn't watching the grill, though; he was watching me, an odd expression on his face as I moved closer. It was one I'd never seen on him before, and one I couldn't decode.

"She likes you," he stated, waving his tongs at her when she started to shimmy and coo in my arms when she saw him.

My shoulder rose. "She's got good taste."

Quentin leaned in to make a face at her, which made both her and me laugh. "She picked pureed peas over apple sauce for breakfast today. Not so sure about this one's personal taste."

Grumbling at him, I shifted the baby onto my hip. She was wiggling and not exactly dainty. "Lily, right?"

127

"That's right." Quentin nodded as he placed the mushrooms on a serving plate. "Almost ten months."

"Not walking, then, yet?"

Quentin glanced over, another bit of surprise on his face. "Not yet, but thank God for that. We can barely keep up with her right now." From the way she was moving and shaking in my arms, I could believe it. "How do you know so much about babies?"

I shifted my weight, my arms already starting to feel tired. "Some of the bands Mom toured with traveled with their families. A few had babies, and I was pretty much the default babysitter."

Quentin closed the grill. "You continue to surprise me."

I bowed my head. "Why, thank you. I'm very astonishing."

"Yeah, kind of like how astonishing it was to learn your mom's band is one of the biggest bands in the world right now." He gave me a sideways look as we headed for the picnic tables that had been lined up together.

And busted.

"Sorry. That's not usually something I brag about to people I just meet. Tends to make them treat me all weird and think I'm cooler than I really am. Then they wind up disappointed after they get to know me."

"Yeah, because you're so disappointing." He motioned at me. "Note the heavy sarcasm in my voice."

"Duly noted," I said, wondering why he was looking at me with so much intensity.

Suddenly the glass door banged open and a line of people filed outside. Aunt Julie and Mrs. Ford were loaded down with salads and bowls of chips, and Mr. Ford was carrying a huge tray of all things meat from his barbecue. Quentin's brothers pretty much slid into their seats like they were practicing for tonight's ball game.

A few more people I didn't recognize emerged from the house, until the benches around the tables were nearly full. Quentin got us two seats when he plopped a couple of grilled mushrooms near his brothers. They quickly backed away, making a cross with their fingers like they were warding off a vampire.

"Mind hanging on to her one more minute? I'm going to grab her high chair real quick." He was already heading for the kitchen.

"Under control," I answered, waving down at the twins, who were sitting across the table from Silas and Abe, blinking at them like they were animals. Actually they did kind of eat like animals, but Mrs. Ford didn't even notice. Aunt Julie, on the other hand, matched her daughters' stares.

"Just in time," Quentin said, carrying a high chair. He attached it to the table, while Lily tried to get ahold of a chunk of my hair and give it a yank.

"Oww," I said, attempting to pry my hair from Lily's death grip.

"Sorry. Should have warned you—Lily loves hair."

By the time I freed my hair from her hand, she'd found another clump with her other one. "You don't say."

"Here, let me take this hair monster before you decide to never come back again." Quentin's arms swooped down to take Lily.

"Please," I tsked, scooping some spinach salad onto my plate when it came around. "It would take a lot more than some baby yanking my hair to scare me away."

"Define a lot more." Quentin paused in the middle of buckling Lily in.

"Oh, I don't know. Some guy forcing me to play baseball when I still bear the emotional scars from my first and only game. I got beaned in the face by a ball."

Quentin winced. "Pitcher out to get you?"

I blinked at him. "I *was* the pitcher."

He covered his mouth, trying to hide his smile. "How is that even possible?"

He was teasing me. He wasn't exactly being subtle about it, either. "Talent," I answered.

"Or lack thereof," he muttered. "But anyone who manages to hit themselves with a ball gets a pass on the baseball game, I guess," he added quickly.

"Thank you."

"You managed to drop a few balls into that carnival game, though," he said, taking a seat.

My eyes lifted. "That's different. That's a carnival game— for fun. Baseball is a sport, the opposite of fun in my book."

Quentin took one of the rolls, poking and smelling it. He still didn't look too sure, but it cracked me up when I saw that his plate mirrored my own. Mushroom, spinach salad, and a vegan roll.

"Can Lily eat this?" he asked, ripping off a little morsel and pinching it.

"Of course. They're only rolls that aren't made with butter or eggs."

Quentin looked doubtful, then took his own bite before breaking off a few small pieces for Lily to work on.

"Not bad," he said as he chewed. "Better than that charred slab of tofu you made me eat last week."

"How would you know? You barely took two bites."

"Two bites too many," he muttered, trying one of the mushrooms. He didn't grimace as he ate it.

"So your mom doesn't work anymore, right? But did she before Lily?" I asked.

"She used to, yeah," Quentin said. "But she took last year off."

"What did she do?" I asked.

"She was a school counselor. She worked at my high school before we moved."

My fork stopped midway to my mouth. I didn't see that one coming. Mrs. Ford wasn't someone I'd feel comfortable approaching for advice on delicate matters.

"Really?"

Quentin made a face. "Really."

"Awkward?" I guessed.

He smiled. "Only extremely."

Lily decided just then that tossing her cup was a better idea than drinking from it. I snagged it from the patio and wiped the mouthpiece off with my napkin. "What does your dad do?"

"He's a software engineer. He mainly does contract jobs, so we can pretty much travel anywhere in the world and he can find a job."

My forehead started to crease. "Why did you guys move, then?" I asked, but that was right when Lily sent her cup sailing again. Into the dirt.

"Warming up for the big game." Quentin bumped his fist against Lily's as he went to retrieve her cup. It was coated in dirt, so he went inside to get another one.

By the time he came back with a new cup, his brothers had already cleared their plates and started setting up the bases for the baseball game. Like Uncle Paul and Aunt Julie, the Fords had a large and level yard. Unlike Uncle Paul and Aunt Julie's yard, it was a space that was used instead of admired, as the bare patches of grass and trampled flowerbeds proved.

"Death Ninjas, you've got five to finish your dinners before a mandatory warm-up!" Silas hollered over at the tables, taking a few practice swings with a bat as long as he was tall.

His dad popped off something about "picking a nicer way to phrase that" while I made it a point to eat as slowly as possible.

"Death Ninjas?"

"Versus the Bonesaw Bruins." Quentin set the clean cup in front of Lily and gave her a look that suggested if she tossed that one into the dirt, she was out of luck.

"I told you, I don't play baseball," I hissed across the table at him as more people started to join his brothers in the yard.

"Clearly. You hit yourself with the ball as the pitcher."

This time, I took a play from Lily's book and sailed a roll in his direction. He just caught it and stuffed it into his mouth, chomping on it as he grinned at me.

"It's baseball with them"—Quentin's eyes drifted to where his brothers had now moved on to using their bats as swords, before leaning across the table—"or fireworks with me."

"Fireworks?"

"You said you wanted an American summer. What's more patriotic than fireworks on the Fourth of July? Well, except maybe baseball."

"Let's go," I said, grabbing my now empty plate before he could change his mind.

That was when Mrs. Ford came up, leaning over Lily as she started unbuckling her from the high chair. "My, my. It appears someone decided to paint themselves with their dinner instead of eating it."

Lily peeked down at herself before looking back at Mrs. Ford, her eyes wide. "Yeah, don't give me that innocent face. Your dad tries the same thing on me and it never works." Mrs. Ford chuckled when Lily started helicoptering her arms as she lifted her from the chair. "But lucky for you, you're much cuter."

Mrs. Ford gave Quentin's head an affectionate pat as she carried Lily inside without a single acknowledgment in my direction. I wasn't sure if no acknowledgment was better than a negative acknowledgment, though.

"Does your mom not like me?" I asked quietly, as gently as I could. I didn't want to offend him or come across as paranoid, but he'd have to be oblivious to not notice the way his mom seemed indifferent toward only one person here tonight.

"She's just protective," Quentin said, distractedly cleaning up the remainders of Lily's dinner.

"Why does she think she needs to protect you from me?"

"I think she's more worried about protecting us from each other." Quentin started to stand, chucking his leftovers in the trash.

"What does that even mean?" I asked, getting up.

"I don't know. She's a high school guidance counselor." Quentin indicated inside, where his mom was wiping down Lily's face. "She's seen some shit, you know?"

I took a moment to consider all the things and situations Mrs. Ford had run across in her line of work. I didn't have to think long. "Okay, I get it," I said, following him into the yard, making sure to give the sparring baseball players a wide berth. "So you've got an overprotective mom, and I've got an underprotective one. That should even us out at least."

Quentin checked over his shoulder at the table. "Yeah, but you've got an *extra*-overprotective aunt."

I watched my aunt eyeing us warily.

"She's seen some shit, too," I said, waving at her. "She's trying to make sure I don't end up exactly like my mom."

Quentin was quiet for a minute as we approached the chairs and blankets he'd apparently set up for our fireworks viewing. He even had a bucket full of candy and snacks.

"Yeah, but your mom turned out pretty okay, right? I mean, she's the lead singer in some huge band, and her daughter is all right, too." He nudged me and motioned at the chairs, letting me take the first pick.

"Well, yeah, but things were pretty rough at the start. Sometimes I think maybe if she had a chance to do it all over again, she might have picked differently, you know?"

"Not everyone has a choice, Jade. Some people have to live with what life throws at them."

I shot him an amused look and put my hands together in

a prayer gesture. "Why, thank you for your wisdom. I didn't realize you life coaches worked on holidays."

Quentin huffed. "Please, that's probably when they're working overtime."

I shook out one of the blankets and spread it on the grass. As I lay down on it, Quentin's head came into view above my face.

"I pulled these chairs from storage, cleaned them off, dragged them out here, and all you needed was a blanket?"

Half of my face creased. "Thank you?"

Sighing, Quentin came around the side, and right when I thought he was about to fall into one of the chairs, he collapsed onto the blanket beside me. Lying down, he inched toward me until our arms touched. There were only a few inches of my skin on his, but that was literally all I could focus on.

Quentin's arm. Quentin's skin. Quentin's warmth.

Before I felt it coming, a shiver trembled down my spine.

"Cold?" he asked. Before I had a chance to answer, his arm wrapped around my head, tucking me closer to him as he drew the blanket across me with his hand.

"Do you like me? As more than just a friend?" It came out suddenly, like I'd been holding it back and it had broken free.

When he took a moment to answer, my head tilted in his direction; his was turned in my direction already. The way he was looking at me—the way his forehead was all creased together—it was as if no one had ever uttered such a stupid question in the history of the world.

"I could answer your question one of two ways." The

corner of his mouth twitched as his face moved closer. "Both ways involve my lips."

His other arm dropping around my waist. "Works for me," I said.

The first shimmering silver firework exploded into the sky, but he didn't notice it. And I wasn't about to acknowledge it.

My eyes closed, waiting for our lips to meet when I heard a very different noise. It wasn't a firework. It was kind of the opposite.

"She's scrubbed down and in her jammies for the night, and since she isn't able to run the bases quite yet . . ." Mrs. Ford was looming above us, with a bouncing Lily in her arms.

I flew up, adjusting and covering and fretting, like she'd caught us doing something way worse than trying for a chaste-ish first kiss. Quentin didn't seem too fazed, though. He just sat up and held out his arms.

"Lily's first Fourth of July. Wouldn't want her to miss her very first fireworks." Mrs. Ford handed a well-loved stuffed bear to Quentin after he'd settled Lily into his lap. She didn't make eye contact with me before she left for the baseball game already under way. Tonight was full of surprises.

"Mr. Snuggles?" I shook one of the bear's arms. Lily was chewing on the other one.

"In the fur and stuffing." Quentin combed Lily's light hair off to the side with his fingers. "Yeah, so, sorry about that." He pulled one of the chairs behind us so we could lean into it and watch the show. "Not exactly the kind of fireworks I had in mind for tonight."

This time, it was my hand that reached for his. Even though he was preoccupied with Lily, his fingers knitted through mine, and he held my hand while he held Lily against his chest so she could watch the show as well.

I smiled over at him, the display in the sky seeming to fade away compared to the view I had of him. "Exactly the kind of fireworks I had in mind."

Chapter Twelve

Grease, chlorine, and BO—that was my eau de perfume of the summer. Hopping in the shower the moment I stepped into the house was all I could think about every day after a shift. I took an extra-long one that afternoon, slipping into a comfy romper after.

The pool had been as busy today as it was yesterday, and Quentin got roped into working until close, which sucked since I'd been hoping to talk with him after our shifts were over.

He said he'd text me when he was done, but that was still a couple hours away. I thought about sitting down in the window seat to journal, but I wasn't feeling especially creative. Waiting on an endless line of kids while suffocating inside the snack shack had a way of draining the inspiration right out of a person. Even *Jane Eyre* couldn't hold my appeal.

Before I knew it, I'd shot off a quick text to Zoey to see if she'd be down to see a band with me in a few weeks. Namely, my dad's band; of course I didn't mention that fact in my invite. Her message pinged back a minute later. She was in.

Score. Zoey was the perfect person to bring with me on

this kind of adventure. She'd be relaxed and supportive, no matter how things went.

With Dad on the brain, I fired up my laptop. Almost a whole twenty-four hours had passed since I'd checked up on him. Let's see what he'd done for his Happy Birthday, America, celebration.

Apparently his Independence Day standard was much lower than the Fords', I thought as I scrolled through the stream of photos in his timeline. His Fourth of July drinks were nothing like the Fords had served.

And what the . . . My nose wrinkled when I scrolled to the next photo. I didn't think it was legal to have half of one's butt hanging from your skirt when in a dining establishment. Even if it was only one that offered hot wings, from the looks of it. Butts on display had to violate some kind of health code.

And what was the guy also known as my dad doing with said ass exhibitionist? Why had he posted half a dozen pictures of the two of them in varying poses that tipped the ew scale?

That was when my phone chimed. I didn't even check the screen before answering, too distracted by the taste of bile in my throat.

"Yay! I got you! The real you and not the voice-recorded or digitized-words version." Mom's voice exploded through the phone so loudly I had to hold it away from my ear.

Just like that, I was smiling again. "Hey, Mom. International time zones really suck."

"They really do," she said, her warm, cheery voice making me feel better hundreds of zip codes away. "How's life?"

At the moment?

"Fabulous," I half-grumbled when my gaze shifted back to my laptop screen. I didn't remember Dad seeming so immature when I'd first tracked him down online. Then again, maybe I'd been too excited about finding him to pay attention to anything else.

"Uh-oh. I know that tone."

Of course she did. She knew every tone in my arsenal.

"I've got a whole box of chocolates sitting in front of me and nowhere to be for three hours. Talk." I could actually hear the sound of packaging being ripped open in the background. She really did have a fresh box of chocolates. Something inside of me kind of ached when I imagined how nice it would be to feel my mom's arm around me as I spilled.

"I just feel off. If that makes any sense at all." I paused, wondering if that was the right way to describe it. "Upside down or something."

Mom was quiet. For half a hot second. "Does a guy have something to do with this kinda off, upside-down feeling?"

My mind drifted to Quentin at the same time my eyes latched onto the next photo of my dad. "Yeah," I answered, not entirely sure which guy had tipped my world slightly off its axis.

Mom tried to muffle her sigh, but I could hear it. "Is he worth it?"

I thought about Quentin. Then I thought about my dad. "Yeah."

"Darn," she said. "Because if he wasn't, that would make my advice so much easier to give you."

"Sorry your only child's inconveniencing you." I grinned and waited. Mom always had good advice—there was never any BS behind it. She just didn't always have a habit of taking her own advice.

"Our world goes wonky for two reasons, Jade." From the sound of it, she was munching on a chocolate right now. Which made me wish I had my own treat. "Either we're changing ourselves or someone is trying to force us to change." There was silence on the line, and then I heard her shift in the background. "You're the only one who knows who you should be, and how to be it."

I chewed on the ends of my fingernails. "Okay. That sounds manageable. Hey, Mom?"

"Hey, Jade?"

I paused, my stomach convulsing when I thought about bringing this up to her. "Do you ever think about him? My dad?" I swallowed, waiting.

She was quiet, and then, "Sometimes."

We were talking about him. Kind of. That was a huge leap compared with me never bringing up his name for fear of life and limb. "Do you ever think about what might have happened if, you know, he hadn't left? If he was still in our lives?"

She was quiet even longer this time, but at least I couldn't hear anything fragile breaking in the background. I heard her long exhale. "Everything happens for a reason. Your dad included."

Everything happens for a reason. That was the phrase that stayed in my head as Mom and I moved on to other topics far less flammable. If that were true, then I was here for a reason, having tracked my dad down and set a date to approach him.

He'd walked away for a reason. And I had mine for wanting to meet him.

Any hesitations that had temporarily arisen were put to bed by the time I hung up with my mom and her box of chocolates. After our two-hour call, I was excited again to meet my dad. So what if his online profile made him seem like a douchebag stuck in his early twenties? He was my dad.

A few minutes after I'd hung up with Mom, Quentin's text came through. He was done with work and had the rest of the night free, which was unusual since he normally had family stuff going on until after nine. He wanted me to come out with him, once again refusing to give any details.

I gave a frustrated groan as I tapped my phone against my knee, debating. My aunt and cousins were gone—I think I remembered her mentioning something about them having some dinner plans tonight—and Uncle Paul might be home sometime tonight, but he sure wouldn't come looking for me first thing.

As I considered, another text came in from Quentin: *Ur only young once.*

Meet u outside in 5, I texted back, noticing my battery was low, but there wasn't time to charge it now. Then I jotted down a quick note to my aunt for when she got home.

Not feeling well. Went to bed early. See you in the morning.

I felt a little guilty when I tacked on the *Love, Jade* part, because I knew I was wrapping up an ugly lie with a pretty bow.

Before I could let the guilt take root, I started to stuff my bed with pillows again, the way I had every night I snuck out of my room. I'd become so good at it, I could do it in under a minute now.

Inspecting my room as I left, I made sure all the lights were off and the curtains were drawn. It was only seven o'clock, so hopefully Aunt Julie and the girls wouldn't be home for a couple more hours. Because note or not, I knew she'd check on me if she came home to discover I was already asleep for the night at seven-thirty.

Closing the door behind me, I rushed down the stairs and dropped the note on the table. Another stab of guilt hit me when I saw the plate of vegan brownies Aunt Julie had left for me. I didn't want to lie to her. I hated it. But if I didn't, how could I experience this summer the way I intended?

Plus, there was the whole thing with my mom practically ordering me to go and have fun this summer or else. Aunt Julie might have been standing in for a couple months, but Mom was my parent. Listening to one was like disobeying the other, but I was going with the commander in chief on this one. And Mom's advice meant getting to see Quentin.

Quentin was waiting for me by his truck. He was leaning into the rusted blue tailgate, hands stuffed into his pockets, staring at me in a way that made my stomach fold in half.

"Little early for sneaking out, isn't it?" he asked when I checked the driveway for the third time, looking for Aunt Julie's minivan. "The sun's still shining and everything."

My hand dropped to my hip as I stopped in front of him. "Little early for you to be free, isn't it? Family duties finish up sooner than expected?"

His shoulders bobbed as he moved around his truck to open the door for me. "I have a free night."

"And you wanted to spend this rare early night of freedom with me?"

"Actually no, but my first and second picks were busy. So you'll have to do." His arms were hanging above the door frame, his face giving nothing away, but his eyes betrayed him.

"Third choice? Lucky me." He laughed. "Third time's the charm?" I said, to which he replied with an overdone frown.

"Come on. You're my first choice. You know I want to spend every night with you." When I stayed turned away from him, he leaned in until his head was tucked right beside mine. "And yes, I mean that in every way you want to translate it."

When I sighed, he laughed again. He kind of loved messing with me. I kind of loved it, too.

"Do you think we can get going?" I checked the back window. Still nothing, but I didn't want to push it.

"Afraid you're going to get caught going somewhere with a friend at seven in the middle of summer?" Before I could respond, he closed the door behind me and loped around to the driver's side.

"Afraid your mom and my aunt shared notes last night." I buckled up as he turned on the engine.

"My mom didn't say anything to your aunt about us hanging out at night."

"How do you know?"

He pulled away from the curb, shrugging. "Because I asked her. From the sound of it, the most personal thing they shared was the secret spice your aunt put in the cherry cobbler."

"Really?" My nose curled. They'd spent most of the night talking. Apparently about nothing of significance.

"Nothing about you being out at night with me came up, I swear."

I had a whole ten seconds to feel relieved, right before the opposite effect set in. My hand curled around the armrest. "That means your mom knows I'm sneaking out, then, right?" When he didn't answer, my head whipped in his direction. "Right?"

His expression answered my question for me. "Maybe?"

"Great. She's going to tell my aunt." I started to pull my phone from my purse to call her and fess up now. She'd probably sit me down and give me a lecture before locking me in my room for the next month and a half, but it would be better coming from me than Quentin's mom.

"No. She's not." Quentin's hand curled around my phone. "She said she wouldn't, so she won't."

"Where are we going?" I asked, not recognizing the road we were on.

"The not knowing's half the fun."

"Yeah, you've pretty much worn that one out by now." I scanned the road for any signs that might give away where he was taking me.

We turned into a parking lot at one of the public beaches a few minutes later. The sun was still setting, but there were a bunch of small fires already going on the beach. And one large one.

Even from here, I could see a swarm of bodies circled around it, closer to thirty than five.

"A bonfire?" I didn't think my voice gave anything away, but Quentin must have picked up on something.

"You wanted to have the quintessential teenage summer. You also just so happen to have picked coastal California for said experiment. You can't get more everyday teen than a beach bonfire. Trust me."

"Is everyone gonna have one of those red Solo cup things?"

He lifted his chin and turned off the engine. "You *know* it."

He met me around the hood of his truck and held his hand out. We'd held hands plenty of times already, so I don't know why this felt like such a big deal, but it did. I guess because Quentin knew some of the people at this bonfire, and I might know a couple from the pool, too. Holding hands when we were alone was different from holding hands in front of a group of people we knew.

It felt like we were announcing ourselves. Like we were making it official.

By the time we were close enough that I could recognize a few familiar faces, it felt like everyone was looking at us. If looking meant staring.

Quentin's head moved closer, his fingers tightening through mine. "And that's how you make an entrance."

That made me smile and feel breathless. It was crazy how he almost always seemed to know what to say or do right when I needed him to.

I waved at Zoey, who winked and made sure I didn't miss the way she was rocking her hips rather inappropriately. I didn't wave at Ashlyn, her pool friend of a friend. She looked as if she was sharpening her claws to better stab me through the heart with them.

A few other lifeguards from the pool had made their way up to Quentin, one of them holding a drink for him that he shook his head at, and the other holding one for me. I took it and started tapping my index finger against the red plastic cup.

Quentin had wrapped up a conversation with them when he nudged me and whispered, "Don't drink that."

I lifted my brow at him. "Just because a person was home-schooled doesn't mean they're clueless."

He waited.

"I know not to actually drink from an open container when someone I barely know hands it to me." Discreetly, I poured the contents into the sand. "Better?"

He smiled. "Better."

After the lifeguards converged on a group of girls who had just arrived, I asked, "Trust issues?"

He steered us through the crowd, lifting his chin at people as they greeted him in passing. "Nah, they're good guys. The only shady substance they put in our cups was the crummy light beer they bought. I only wanted to make sure you're as street-smart as you are book-smart."

"My mom is probably the most street-smart person you'll ever meet. Believe me, she made sure her daughter knows what's up."

"Now, I know that's not true," he replied.

"Why's that?"

Quentin's eyes flashed at me. "Because if you were smart, you wouldn't be spending time with a guy like me."

"Being smart doesn't have anything to do with why I'm spending time with you," I said, unfazed. "I've got a bunch of community service hours I want to complete this summer."

He huffed. "Aren't you an all-around Mother Teresa?"

Most of the people were standing clustered in small groups, but we decided to take a seat in the sand. It was warm from the sun and the fire, and I wiggled my toes into it, already enjoying my very first beach bonfire. The company to my left might have been the main reason for that, but the warm sand and the sound of the ocean didn't hurt, either.

"If you want a drink, I'll get you one, but you know, don't feel like you have to drink just because everyone else is."

I nudged him. "Not everyone."

He kicked his sandals off and buried his toes beside mine. "I don't drink. But I don't mind if you do."

"Like you don't drink ever, or you don't drink anymore?"

He scooted us back a few feet when a couple of guys started tossing fresh wood on the already massive fire.

"Anymore."

"Reason?" I dropped my head in front of him when he stayed quiet.

"I didn't make the best decisions when I used to drink, and I already make enough bad decisions without the alcohol, so I don't mess with it anymore."

"Define bad decisions."

He groaned, but it was one of those good-natured groans. "You're not usually so curious."

My palm turned up. "Indulge me."

He shook his head. "Let's see, there was the time I went streaking through my old high school's football field during halftime." When I blinked, he added, "I had a gorilla mask on and had my hand over my . . . you know."

"Then that's not streaking."

His head cocked. "Then what is it?"

"Jogging semi-exposed."

Quentin rolled his eyes at me. "Fine. But I was hauling ass, not jogging, and I was *mostly* exposed, save for what was hidden by a palm and a few fingers."

"Please," I said, blowing out a breath. "That's one citizen exercising his right to freedom of expression. I wouldn't put that in the not-the-best-decision category."

"And then there was the time I jumped off a twenty-foot cliff into the lake below because my buddies who'd already done it were daring me to."

"Wow. So *you're* the person all those moms were talking about. Nice to put a face to the name."

I circled my hand, suggesting I was waiting for more, but he just shrugged. "And other stuff."

Right as I was about to ask him to clarify what "other stuff," I noticed someone approaching. Quentin's whole face changed.

"Oh my gosh, it *is* you." The girl beamed, moving closer. "Quentin, *no way.*"

I was too busy staring at her to see the look on his face, but I could hear the catch in his voice. "Hey, Lindsey. How's it going?" He started to stand, but she'd already dropped on the sand beside us.

"Hi, I'm Lindsey," she said to me, smiling instead of sharpening her claws, so I guessed I was safe.

"Hi," I said, glancing back at Quentin. Yeah, something definitely wasn't right. "Jade."

"Cool skirt." Her eyes dropped to the patterned maxi skirt I was wearing. "Urban Outfitters?"

I expected Quentin to give a little laugh, but his face was frozen.

"Thrift store in Denmark," I told her.

She laughed a little, like I'd made a joke. She was dressed differently than the rest of the girls at the bonfire. More polished or put together or something.

"So how have things been?" Lindsey asked Quentin, her eyes just sympathetic enough for me to assume she had an idea things might be a little rough.

Which confused me. Why was she behaving like she was talking to someone who'd just lost his dog?

"Good," Quentin answered eventually, clearing his throat. "How 'bout you?"

"Same. Good." Insert long, awkward pause. "I can't believe we're going to be seniors this year, can you?"

Quentin shook his head stiffly. "Me either."

"Last year wasn't the same without you at school. It was so weird." Lindsey smiled, like she was reliving a memory. "Way too mellow for my taste."

He stared into the fire, appearing tense. His back looked ready to snap from the tension. "I bet."

Insert second awkward silence here.

"How's the family?" Lindsey asked as her eyes roamed the party.

"Good," he answered again, sniffing.

"And how's—"

"Everyone's good, Lindsey." Quentin cut her off, his gaze flicking toward her. "Thanks for checking."

I felt like the shiny silver ball in those old pinball machines.

No clue what was going on or where this conversation was heading next.

Right when it looked like Lindsey was about to get up and leave, she sighed. "Have you talked to Blaire?"

The name made Quentin's jaw look ready to break through the skin. "There's nothing to talk about."

Lindsey nodded, almost like she understood. "I'm sorry for how everything went down. That was cold. Even for Blaire."

A sharp exhale came from Quentin. "I wasn't surprised at all."

Lindsey gave a small nod, her eyes going a little sad. Then she leaned over and gave Quentin the quickest hug ever. "Good luck, Quentin."

He just sat there, unmoving.

"Nice to meet you, Jade. Do me a favor and look after him for me." Lindsey lifted her chin in Quentin's direction. "He's one of the good ones."

I waved at her. "I know."

Lindsey disappeared into the crowd while I gave Quentin a chance to cool down. I didn't have a clue what had just happened, but I knew it was something big.

"I know what you're thinking." He cleared his throat, his head turning toward me.

"I doubt it."

He gave me a look. "What the hell just happened? Right?"

I drew lines in the sand with my finger. "Okay, so you know what I'm thinking."

His face was starting to relax. The rest of his body was, too. "Can you guess what I'm thinking right now?"

My fingers rolled across the sand. "That you're dying to tell me?"

He rubbed at the back of his neck. "Not even close."

"Quentin—"

"This isn't the place, Jade." His jaw moved as his gaze wandered toward the bonfire and everyone circled around it.

A flash of frustration went through me. One minute I thought we were making progress, the next I felt like we were going backward.

Before I could press him any harder, someone plopped onto the sand beside me.

"Sorry. Am I interrupting?" Zoey's smile fell when she saw the way Quentin and I were in some kind of stare-down.

"Perfect timing, actually." Quentin rose from the sand, dusting off his backside. "I better go intervene before someone lights themselves or someone else on fire." He made his way toward the cluster of lifeguards aiming a can of lighter fluid at the bonfire and intercepted them. Alcohol and lighter fluid should not mix. Ever.

"I totally just interrupted something, didn't I?" Zoey's nose crinkled as she messed with the bow she'd tied in her hair.

"It's okay. He won't get out of it that easily, trust me."

"Good." Zoey nudged me as she flagged someone over. "I wanted to introduce you to someone. My friend who's a friend of . . ." Her gaze swept across the bonfire where Ashlyn was working the crowd of guys around her. She'd probably spent two whole hours on her makeup tonight—at least all that effort was paying off.

"This is Lindsey—"

Lindsey and I exchanged a smile. "Yeah, we just met," I said as she settled onto the sand again.

"Nice to meet you. For the second time." Lindsey laughed.

"So do you guys go to the same school or something?" I asked.

Zoey shook her head. "No. Lindsey goes to Murray Park; I go to Edison. The same one Quentin goes to."

He was still distracted, trying to keep his friends from fulfilling their pyro dreams. In the bunch, I noticed the girl from the carnival with the "obscured" heart. Beside her, a leggy girl with beach hair had an arm draped behind her neck. Sam the surfing buddy, I assumed.

If Quentin wasn't going to answer my questions, maybe someone else would.

"Quentin used to go to your school, though, right? With Blaire?" I asked Lindsey.

"That's right. Ashlyn goes there, too." Lindsey curled her legs beneath her, getting comfortable.

Perfect. Since I only had a few hundred questions to run by her.

"Who's Blaire?" Zoey piped in, her head moving between the two of us.

I stayed quiet. But so did Lindsey.

Which only had my something-is-wrong radar hit peak levels. This Blaire topic wasn't just a land mine for Quentin.

It was like he had telepathy or something, because two seconds later he was at my side, hovering above us.

"Jade, can you help me with something?" Quentin said, ducking back into the conversation.

"Yeah, we were just leaving anyway, to give you some alone time," Zoey said, linking arms with Lindsey and pulling her up. "Too much couple drama going on for my taste."

"What drama?" I asked.

Zoey's finger moved between Quentin and me. "Whatever drama neither of you two are willing to get out in the open."

I shot her a weird look, waving good-bye to Lindsey for the second time that night.

"What's the matter?" I exhaled, feeling my stomach drop when I noticed the way he was looking at me.

"Nothing's the matter." His head gestured to the ocean. "I was just thinking how it's a perfect night for a swim."

Shiny silver ball thing feeling times two.

"A swim," I said flatly.

"There is the biggest ocean in the world right behind us, waiting. It's a warm summer night. You want to live like a red-blooded American teenager." His foot tapped my leg, his smile more crooked than straight. "You're only young once."

"Not even touching on the fact that you're so avoiding trying to explain what happened earlier." I raised my hand and gave him a look that suggested I wasn't going to let it go because I was willing to delay the inevitable. "But you're right. I do want to *live* like one of those red-blooded teenagers. Live. Not die drowning in that biggest ocean in the world."

Quentin lowered his hand for me to take. "If you're worried about drowning, you're swimming with the right person."

I dropped my hand in his and let him pull me up. "Whatever you say, Head Lifeguard Ford."

Chapter Thirteen

As we walked down to the water, it didn't take long before darkness soaked in around us. It took my eyes a second to adjust, but I kept moving forward, letting Quentin lead the way.

By the time we'd made it to where the waves were more roar than echo, Quentin stopped. When he started to tug his shirt off, I took a step back and tried not to stare.

He must have mistaken my dazed look for something else. "If you don't want to swim, it's okay. It was just an idea. I'm not going to force you." His hand molded around my arm, rubbing it lightly like he was trying to calm or reassure me.

It took turning so I was facing the ocean to be able to form coherent sentences. "Who wouldn't want to swim in that ginormous black"—I paused, a scene from *Jaws* flashing through my mind—"dangerous ocean at night?"

"See?" He grinned, waving an arm between him and me. "You get me."

Dropping his shirt in the sand, he held out his hand again to lead me the rest of the way to the water. "Come on," he said when I didn't take it. "We'll only get our feet wet. See how we feel after that."

But I didn't only want to get my feet wet—not if I was going to do this. I wanted to fully submerge myself in that thrilling, terrifying mass. Because who would want a drop when they could have the whole ocean?

"What"—Quentin's voice caught when he saw what was happening—"are you doing?"

My tank wound up on top of his shirt. He kind of blinked at the two tops like he was working on a differential equation.

"Going swimming." I shrugged as my hands moved to my skirt.

Quentin's hand flew into the air like he was a crossing guard trying to stop a garbage truck barreling down the road. "I meant swimming, as in the clothed version."

I pointed at my bralette. "I am clothed," I said, kicking my long skirt over to the growing pile of clothes. "There. Ready to swim." I held out my arms like I was the very picture of cool and confident, but I was pretty much the opposite. Especially with the way he was staring at me.

"You're in your underwear." He said it like he was confused. Like he thought he knew what was going on but couldn't quite convince his brain of what his eyes were telling him.

"You said you wanted to go for a swim, and I really don't want to sink to the bottom of the ocean floor because of a skirt with fifty yards of fabric."

"But *underwear*."

My hands went to my hips. "If it makes you feel better, we

can call it my 'swimsuit.' Besides, this 'swimsuit' covers more real estate than most of the ones I've seen at the pool."

I started to move toward the water. "Are we swimming or what?" He jogged to catch up. "You're not really letting me swim in my underwear alone, are you?" When I glanced back, he'd definitely been checking out my butt.

I think it was the way my eyes dropped to his shorts, more than my words, that made him realize what I was getting at.

He came to a stop, his fingers already working the top button of his shorts free. "Who's the bad influence now?" He winked up at me before sending his shorts flying back to where the rest of our clothes were.

I tried not to make it seem like I was checking him out, but he was right. I could kid myself all I wanted—it didn't change the fact that he was sliding up beside me, wearing nothing but his underwear. Boxers definitely were *not* a swimsuit.

"Just our feet at first, right?" I jolted when I felt the first wash of cold ocean water touch my toes.

"Of course," he said, like I had no reason to doubt him. And then his arms were around me as he threw me over his shoulder, charging into the water as fast as he could.

I barely had a chance to scream and thump his back a few times before he'd gotten deep enough to dunk us both.

I came up sputtering. We both swallowed so much salt water, I felt part ocean. But we were having so much fun, I didn't even think about how dark the water was or what scary ocean animals might have been lurking nearby. I didn't feel how cold it was or how I was swimming, in my underwear, with some boy who was in his underwear, too. In the Pacific Ocean. At night.

So this was what I'd been missing out on. I got it now. What the big deal was. I loved my life on the road with my mom. It was part of me, ingrained into everything I was. But this . . . this might be part of me, too.

I didn't realize I was shaking and chattering until Quentin touched my jaw. He stopped splashing and trying to dunk me, his face taking on a concerned shadow. "You're cold?"

Now that I was thinking about it . . . "Only a little."

He held his arms open and came closer. It wasn't the first time I'd seen Quentin wet. It wasn't the first time I'd seen him in a "swimsuit." But from the way my throat was going all dry and parched, it was like this was the first everything.

"Good thing I'm hot," he said, right before he folded his arms around me, one at a time, and drew me close to his body.

I snuggled against him, the next tremble that spilled down me from something other than cold. "Only a little," I said.

His body rocked against mine from his laughter. "A bad influence and an ego checker? I think I'm smitten."

"Yeah." My head shook against him as I pressed a little closer. "Me too."

I could feel the way his chest was rising and falling quickly against mine. My thoughts drifted to last night and what had almost happened.

Tonight there were no overprotective moms or aunts or anyone to interrupt us. Tonight there was only him and me.

When I leaned my head back so I was looking up at him,

I knew he was thinking the same thing. His hands curled around my back, drawing me somehow closer. The water from his hair dripped down his face, rolling past his lips, and I wasn't sure I'd ever experience a more perfect kiss than this one—waist-deep in the ocean.

My arms circled behind his back as my thumbs dragged down the dip of his spine. This time, he was the one who trembled. When I pushed a little closer, I could feel the warmth from his skin sinking into mine. His chest was moving faster now, his gaze dropping to my mouth as I felt his fingers comb into the ends of my wet hair.

Quentin's head was dropping toward mine, his glowing green eyes excited, and one moment later something rushed over me. It wasn't that warm, happy feeling I was expecting to feel. It was pretty much the other kind.

The wave hit us at the same time, taking us both by surprise. One second I was upright, and the next I was being swirled beneath the surface until I'd smashed up onto the beach. It took me a minute to catch on to what happened, but that was when I noticed Quentin a little ways down from me, in the same position as I was, stretched across the beach, laughing like we'd gotten off some awesome new ride at Six Flags.

"Are you okay?" He was still laughing, but crawling down toward me, concern settling into his expression when he saw I wasn't moving.

"I don't even know how to answer that right now." I sat up on my knees and shook my head, feeling like a liter of salt water and sand was running from my ears.

Quentin rushed beside me and hoisted me up, sliding the hair away from my cheek and brushing the sand off it. "I don't see any physical injuries."

I gave him a light shove when I caught him checking me out. But not necessarily for injuries.

Glancing down, I made sure everything was still covered that should have been. Good. Mostly, I thought, adjusting one side of my bralette.

"That's twice now something has gotten in the way of me trying to kiss you," he said, smoothing another chunk of my hair away.

"Think fate's trying to tell you something?" I ran my thumb across his cheek where a smear of sand had coated him.

"Yeah, I think it is."

My head tilted, waiting.

His forehead dropped to mine. "Try harder."

I stifled my smile as he took my hand and led me back up the beach.

"Or it could be trying to tell us—"

"Nope, definitely not that," he interrupted, heading toward the pile of clothes.

"Why not that?"

"Because we're great together, Jade Abbott." He motioned between us. "Just look at us."

I studied him. Coated in sand, boxers pasted to his body and twisted around his legs. I wasn't any better. Pasted in said sand, hair a tangled knot around my neck, covered in goose bumps.

"We are pretty damn great together," I said, about to start

laughing with him, but I stopped when we got to the piles of clothes. Something was missing.

My clothes.

"Um. Where did my skirt and top go?" I checked the immediate area, hoping maybe a gust of ocean air had tumbled them off a ways.

"I don't know. They were right here." Quentin let go of my hand and started wandering the beach, looking for them. "Mine are still here. That's weird." His hands settled on his hips as he stopped.

As I frantically searched farther up the beach, something caught my eye: Ashlyn's distant figure in the bonfire shadows, and a moment when I swore I could almost see the last scrap of my skirt being consumed by the flames.

"I think I know where my clothes went." My arms wound around my stomach, not sure what I felt more—anger or panic.

"Where?" Quentin came up beside me, waiting for me to point them out.

Instead, I indicated the party. "Someone added a little fuel to the fire."

It only took Quentin a moment to get it. He must have seen her, too, standing there looking victorious like she'd conquered the Roman Empire.

He grabbed his clothes and held them toward me. "Here. I know they'll be huge on you, but at least they're dry and provide coverage."

"What are you going to wear?" I shook my head, refusing to take them.

He motioned down at his wet boxers. When I sighed, he held his arms out. "What? It's my 'swimsuit.'"

"If you're using that kind of logic, then this is mine."

Quentin's throat moved when we took another look at my "swimsuit." "Yeah, but yours covers a lot less than mine. And I don't want anyone else seeing you in it."

I bit my lip. "I can't believe some chick burned my clothes because I showed up to a bonfire with you."

Quentin started scrunching up his tee like he was going to put it on me if I didn't do it. "You did want the full teenage experience, right?"

I let him tug it over my head, winding my arms through the armholes. "I'm wondering if it's not too late to order the three-quarter portion."

He winked at me, sweeping the shirt down my body. I pulled his shorts up to my waist. Even after he cinched the belt as tight as it would go, they were still kind of falling off me, but it worked.

I held out the sides of the tee. "I think I could fit three of me in here."

He was trying not to laugh as he took a good look at me. "Not so fast. I can barely keep up with one of you." He wound his arm behind my shoulders as we started up the beach. "Let's get you home before a strong gust of wind comes and blows you all the way to Australia."

"Why are we heading to the bonfire instead of the parking lot?" I asked, coming close to sighing from the warmth of his dry clothes. I hadn't realized how cold I'd gotten.

"I have to do something real quick."

Ashlyn could see us now, but hers wasn't the only attention

we had by the time we finished trudging through the sand. Some of the guys were giving Quentin an approving look, and most of the girls were busy checking him out, which was kind of fantastic because no one was looking at me.

"Nice outfit." I guess someone was looking at me.

I shrugged at Ashlyn, reminding myself to stay calm.

"Thanks" was all I said.

She blinked at me like I was clueless, and maybe I was where cattiness was concerned.

Quentin squared himself in front of Ashlyn. "Next time you want to burn someone's clothes, burn mine. Leave Jade out of it."

Ashlyn angled herself at Quentin. Her eyes narrowed when she saw the way he was holding my hand—like there was nothing anyone could do to tear it away. "What? Are you going to threaten me if I don't?"

"Absolutely not."

She stared him down as her arms crossed. "Just trying to warn her to be careful of who she hangs out with. Nothing but trouble follows those who get involved with you." There was a moment's pause, then her eyes flashed. "Just ask Blaire."

Quentin was quiet for two heartbeats. Then he looked her in the eye. "I don't need to ask Blaire anything. I know exactly what she thinks about what went down. She's made that really damn obvious."

Ashlyn's face went kind of blank, like she was trying to process this. I didn't see what happened after because Quentin was already leading me away from the party, ignoring the catcalls and whistles some of his friends were firing his way.

"Jade!" a voice called behind us.

It was Zoey, jogging to us, holding up something of mine I'd forgotten all about. "Oh my gosh," I said. "Thank you." I took my phone from her with a sigh of relief. The battery was dead, but at least my phone was still in one piece.

"Yeah, I managed to snag that away from her before it went in with your clothes." Zoey paused, her nose crinkling. "I'm sorry about that. I would have saved the rest, too, if I'd realized what she was doing five seconds sooner." She sighed, like she was to blame. "Some friend, right?"

I shook the phone at her, not missing that in rescuing it for me she'd probably made an enemy of Ashlyn. Pulling her into a quick hug, I said, "Some friend."

After that, Quentin and I headed for his truck.

We didn't say anything as we drove away from the lot. He stared out the windshield, cranked on the heater until the truck felt like a sauna, and tossed me his charger. I plugged in my phone and waited for it to power up.

"Who's Blaire?" I asked when we were a few minutes from home.

Quentin glanced over at me; his face read *Really?* When I stayed silent, he knew I wasn't letting it go this time.

"She was my girlfriend at my old school." He sounded like a robot, scripted and stilted.

"A serious one, or not really?" I continued.

He cracked his neck. "Pretty serious."

I bit my lip, knowing he did not want to talk about this, but I had to know. "But not serious anymore, right?"

He grunted. "God, no."

I turned in my seat so I was facing him. "What happened?"

I'd never seen so many emotions play out on a person's face all at once.

It was at least a full minute later before he replied, "Life happened."

My hands curled into fists. "That's not an answer, Quentin."

"She saw things one way. I saw them another," Quentin said curtly. "So we went our separate ways."

Before I could press any further, we'd turned onto our street. We hadn't rolled up to the curb yet, but I knew something was wrong. Lights were on inside my aunt and uncle's house, and I could make out their shadows pacing behind the curtain in the big picture window. I also didn't miss another window that was all lit up—mine. As if on cue, my phone blared to life then, and a whole mess of missed calls and texts came in. All of them from my aunt—all of them frantic. I was in so much trouble.

"I'll walk you in and explain." Quentin was already starting to open his door, but I grabbed his arm.

"No!" I shouted, scanning his still-wet boxers, which had somehow crept even higher up his legs on the drive home. "It will be better if it's just me." My head started to spin at the mere thought of explaining this to them. "And this is so, so bad."

I knew right away what conclusion my aunt would jump to.

"Listen, let me talk to them. I'm sure they'll be okay once they know what happened."

My eyebrows hit my hairline. "This is my aunt we're

talking about. The woman whose main fear is I could get pregnant and forever ruin my life if a boy looks at me wrong."

Quentin sighed, rubbing at his forehead. "We went to a bonfire at the beach. We didn't drink. Hell, we didn't even kiss, damn my best efforts, and we're home before eleven o'clock." He thrust his hand at the time showing on his truck's radio dial. "How is that being irresponsible and reckless and attempting to ruin your life?"

"You're in your underwear, Quentin! And I'm pretty sure they'll notice these aren't my clothes!"

I winced when I watched my aunt throw her arms in the air. "I'm going to spend the next month and a half getting reamed for the sneaking out before I even get a chance to explain what we did tonight."

"Yeah, maybe you should have just told them you were leaving instead of going behind their backs in the first place." Quentin leaned around me so he had a view of the scene inside.

"Sure, then they would have locked me inside of that room for the summer and thrown away the key." My hand lowered to the door handle, knowing I was only delaying the inevitable. "I'll text you later. If I still have my phone privileges, which I probably won't." When I threw the door open and climbed out, his face fell.

He put his truck into gear hesitantly, like he wasn't sure he should let me do this on my own.

He was still there when I climbed the front stairs and went to grab the key my aunt kept hidden under one of her flowerpots. I didn't need it, though.

The door flung open, and I was met by both my aunt and

uncle, gaping at me like I'd showed up on a motorcycle with a cigarette hanging from my lips.

"Where in God's name have you been?" Uncle Paul was the first to speak, thrusting his arm at me to get inside or else. I wasn't sure what *or else* was. I was in uncharted territory.

"I was at the beach," I said, feeling about one millimeter tall from the way my aunt was looking at me. Her eyes were all red and puffy, like she'd spent the past few hours sobbing. "It was a bonfire, and a bunch of people were there."

"A bonfire? A bunch of people?" Uncle Paul's face was insanely red. His eyes looked ready to pop out of his head, and veins were bulging in his neck. "And why are you dressed like you're in some kind of gang?" Uncle Paul motioned at my outfit, shirt down to almost my knees, shorts about ready to fall off me, like I was guilty of some kind of crime.

"I went for a swim," I started, pausing to decide how to best explain what came after that. "Then my clothes kind of disappeared and someone was nice enough to lend me theirs."

I thought I'd done a decent job explaining the whole thing. However, every word from my mouth made my aunt's and uncle's mouths fall open ever farther.

"Let me see if I have this right, because I don't do my best logical thinking when the niece I'm responsible for has disappeared without letting me or her aunt know." Uncle Paul was pacing now, yanking at his tie like it was choking him. "You took off your clothes to go swimming?"

Since everything I was saying was only pissing him off, I went with body gestures instead.

When I nodded, he continued. "So I assume you must have planned accordingly and brought a swimsuit with you."

My teeth sank into my lower lip as I lifted my shoulders. Uncle Paul's face went full-on scarlet.

"Am I to take it that you went swimming, in your underwear, with a 'bunch of people'?"

"No! No way!" I answered as soon as I realized what he was getting at. "I only went swimming with one person. Everyone else was still at the bonfire. Way far away."

Instead of my explanation putting his worries at ease, it went the other direction. "Was this one person a girl? Or a boy?"

My aunt was covering her mouth with her hands, and my uncle was tugging at his tie again.

"No, it wasn't like that! It was—"

"It was with me, Mr. Davenport." And there was Quentin, still wet from our swim, still in nothing but his boxers. "Jade went swimming with me."

My eyes closed, knowing that as much as Quentin thought this would help, it was only going to make it about a million times worse.

"You're the new boy a few houses down, right?"

Quentin nodded, stepping farther inside. "That's right."

"You think you can take advantage of some innocent girl, have your fun, then break her heart when you've gotten what you want? Or worse, leave her pregnant and alone, with no way to take care of herself or the baby?"

"Uncle Paul," I hissed, a serious defensive edge hitting me.

Quentin stood up straighter, not blinking as he stared at my uncle. "That's not the kind of person I am at all."

Uncle Paul snorted, like that was a joke.

"I've seen you all of twenty minutes all summer, Uncle

Paul." I stepped forward so I was in front of him. "You don't get to yell at Quentin and accuse him of terrible things when you don't know him, and you don't get to yell and accuse me of things when you haven't taken the time to get to know me, either. So don't you dare lecture me on responsibility." Now came the tears. They stung my eyes as they rolled to my cheeks. "I wasn't doing anything wrong or illegal, or anything that would put me in the same situation as my mom."

Uncle Paul spit out each word. "You snuck out of the house, Jade. You left a note saying you went to bed, made it look like you were in bed when your aunt went up to check on you, and ignored our calls when we tried to work out where you'd disappeared to." Uncle Paul held up the note I'd left on the table, like it was my guilty verdict. "How is that not doing anything wrong?"

"I—no, you're right. I shouldn't have done that, and I'm sorry, but I didn't do what you think I was doing tonight." My eyes slid toward Quentin, who had to bite the inside of his cheek to stay quiet. "I shouldn't have snuck out, but I knew you wouldn't have let me go if I told you I was going with Quentin." When I turned toward my aunt, I found her sitting on the edge of the couch, staring at the carpet like she was lost and didn't have a map. "I'm sorry."

She nodded, then her eyes lifted to mine. "You were supposed to watch the girls tonight." She paused, letting that settle between us. It only took a moment for my stomach to twist into knots with that feeling of suddenly remembering something that was really super-important. "Your uncle and I were going to go to dinner and a show. I asked you last week if you'd mind watching the twins and you said you would."

Suddenly, I realized my aunt was dressed up. She had on a pair of heels. There was even a bouquet of roses Uncle Paul must have brought her. I didn't have to check her calendar to know how long it had been since Uncle Paul had taken her on a date. And I was the one responsible for ruining this one for them. Ruining it for her.

"I forgot." It came out like a whisper. I'd always been so responsible, so organized, and had never, ever forgotten something this important before. "I'm so sorry, Aunt Julie. I can't believe—"

"Wait." Quentin moved into view, his brows drawn together. "So you were supposed to be watching your cousins tonight?" He waited, like he needed me to confirm it one more time.

My head moved slightly as my vision went blurry from the tears. "I forgot. I totally forgot all about it."

"You can't just forget about that kind of stuff, Jade. They're little kids—they're your family. If you say you're going to be there for them, you better mean it." Now it seemed like he was the one scolding me, looking at me like I'd let him down in every way, too. "You can't bail on your responsibilities like that."

I pressed my palms into my eyes and shook my head. What was going on? Why was he so mad at me, too?

"I know, Quentin. I know. I wasn't trying to forget. It wasn't like I meant to do this."

He shook his head, backing up toward the front door. "That doesn't give you a pass, Jade. Someone was counting on you to be there. And you weren't. The why doesn't matter."

He didn't say anything else. He didn't wave good-bye or flash his middle finger or even look at me, which was somehow worse. He just walked away, leaving me behind to figure out what the hell was going on. Not just in his life this time, but in mine.

Chapter Fourteen

So, grounded. A new concept for me, and one I didn't want to get very familiar with.

After the night I let my aunt, my uncle, and clearly Quentin down, I thought I'd at least have one person in my corner. Not so much. Mom didn't give me quite the earful Uncle Paul and Aunt Julie had, but I got the most serious "talking to" from her yet. When I rallied by reminding her that she was the one who told me to really put myself out there this summer and get into a little trouble, she cut me off and said a little trouble was swimming in my underwear in a girlfriend's backyard pool. A *lot* of trouble was sneaking out of the house, swimming in the ocean in my underwear with some boy I'd met a month ago, and ignoring the panicked calls and texts from my aunt.

So yeah. At least I had a clear definition of what a little and a lot of trouble were. That would make things simpler for when the next century came and I was finally allowed a sliver of freedom.

Work was the only time I'd been allowed to leave the

house this week, and it was all kinds of sad when I couldn't wait to work a six-hour shift sweating and scooping.

Quentin and I'd been working different shifts this week, so I'd only seen him one time when I was leaving the pool on Lemon the kinda-bike and he was arriving in his truck. He didn't see me when I gave a little wave. Or he pretended not to see me—I wasn't sure.

I didn't know what to make of that whole situation. He'd been cool about everything. He'd come storming into my aunt and uncle's living room in his boxers to have my back, for crying out loud, but then he seemed to switch sides when he discovered I forgot about babysitting. I mean, I was disappointed in myself and felt like crap over it, but it wasn't something I'd expected him to be all opinionated about. Maybe it was because he was used to babysitting for his siblings and couldn't comprehend simply forgetting about a night. Maybe it was for any other reason, but I'd never know if he didn't talk to me.

After the first and only text I sent him the next morning—to say sorry and check in—went unanswered, I took the hint and was trying to leave him alone. But I couldn't bring myself to regret our swim and our second almost-first kiss. How did we get from that dip in the ocean to here?

"Oh, yay. My fan club's here," I muttered to Zoey. I tried to ignore the trio of girls making their entrance, but they weren't doing the same. Their goal was to make me as uncomfortable as possible it seemed.

Zoey sighed, in the middle of ringing up a mom with five kids staging mayhem around her. "Ashlyn's relentless. Whether it's someone she wants or someone she wants to destroy."

I fired a tight smile at her as I worked on the order. "Thanks for the pep talk. You always know exactly what to say to make me feel better."

Zoey handed back change to the mom, who looked like she was already counting down the minutes to bedtime despite it only being eleven in the morning. I was right there with her.

I chose to ignore the glowers from Ashlyn's crew. Luckily my shift was almost over. It was strange how my shifts seemed to fly by now that they were the only measure of freedom I had. It was really strange how much I found myself wishing Janet would break down and beg me to stay a few extra hours.

My shift had been over for five minutes, but I was lingering, wiping down counters I'd already cleaned twice. Zoey must have noticed I was stalling, because she removed the spray bottle from my hand.

"Dude. You're off the clock. Why the manic-obsessive cleaning?"

My eyes darted to the clock hanging above the door. He was never late for work.

Realization dawned on her face. "He switched his shifts around. You know, in case you were wondering," she added when I gave her a look.

"Why did he do that?" I asked, like she'd have a clue.

She bit her lip. "I kinda thought you'd know more about that than me."

I leaned into the counter, feeling deflated and confused. "He's avoiding me."

"You think?" Zoey pretended to be really busy after that.

"Did he say anything to you?"

She shook her head. "No. It just seems like, you know, something's up between you two. But I hope you work it out, whatever it is. You guys seemed good for each other."

My world felt even more upside down than before, but I caught myself smiling. "Thanks, Zoey." When I moved in to give her a hug, she laughed and hugged me back. I'd made friends all over the world, but this was different. Time made a difference in the depth of friendships, and I was starting to understand what I'd been missing by spending my life on the road—friendships that went beyond the realm of a laugh and a good time.

Before I left the pool, I checked the updated schedule and saw that Quentin had exchanged his two-to-six shift for Zach's three-to-seven. I wondered if the switch had anything to do with mine ending at two. Or two-ten, by the time I actually forced myself to leave.

Aunt Julie knew my schedule and how long it took me to bike from work to home, which meant I'd have to haul if I didn't want to get the Grand Inquisition for getting home five minutes late.

Ugh. Being grounded was the worst.

By the time I made it back to the house, I was actually dripping sweat. I could feel it rolling down my temples and everything. Time for a shower and a whole lot of nothing else for the rest of the day. I was really looking forward to it. Or not.

When I came in from the garage, Aunt Julie was sitting at the kitchen table kind of just frozen, staring at the wall across from her like she was having a conversation with it.

"Jade?" she said, coming out of her trance. She twisted in her chair. "How was work?"

"Great. Highlight of my day," I said. "If you'll excuse me, I'm off to my cell for the rest of the day. I mean my room."

"Jade . . ."

"It's okay, Aunt Julie. I messed up. I get it."

"We're both trying to figure this out, you know?" she said as I was leaving the kitchen. "We should talk about this. . . ."

"I'll be in my room if you need me."

"You want to go to the grocery store with the girls and me after I pick them up from their violin lesson?" she asked.

I felt a pang of guilt. She'd trusted me, and I'd thought I was a trustworthy person, but now I wasn't sure. "I'm okay, but thanks." I hurried up the stairs before she could ask me if I wanted to peel carrots with her at the sink later. She was trying to connect, trying to make amends after our blowup in the living room, but I wasn't sure if I was ready to be forgiven.

Following a shower, I read for a bit, and wrote for a while after dinner. Mom had tried calling me a few times, but I let it go to voicemail. After the third unanswered call, she gave up and sent a text.

Love you no matter what was all it said. And I bawled like a baby. I'd been mad at Mom for siding with my aunt and uncle. She was *my* mom, she was supposed to be on my side always, and she'd been the one practically ordering me to make the most of this summer and not spend it shut up in some room reading and writing the way I was now. It was her big idea for me to get into trouble, and then she'd acted like I'd broken every law in the book because of it.

Not answering her calls was my pitiful way of letting her know I was upset. Her still calling and texting to say she loved me was her way of letting me know she didn't care how angry I was with her.

It was after nine when my hand finally gave out on me and no more words could be penned without risking it falling off. It was a nice night, so I opened the window to let in some fresh air. As I looked around, I couldn't help glancing down the block.

The Fords' house seemed unusually quiet. Especially for a Friday night. The yard didn't look like a toy store had thrown up all over it, and there was only one light on in the house, instead of one in every room.

Quentin's truck was in the driveway, but Mrs. Ford's SUV wasn't. Maybe the family was out doing something. Maybe they were going to move, since they couldn't stand the idea of living so close to someone as irresponsible as me.

I was so busy wallowing in self-pity, I almost didn't notice the familiar form moving outside, wrestling with what looked like a car seat. I stretched farther from the window. Quentin was on the phone. I could just make out a few words, and they were anxious-sounding. Something about Lily and the ER before he rushed back inside the house.

I made an impulsive decision. One of those where there's not a lot of thought given to it, just a lot of action. The panic in his voice scared me. I'd never seen him anything less than calm—not even when he was rescuing that boy from the pool.

I didn't realize I'd forgotten to put on shoes until I'd already reached the rain gutters, and by that point there was no way I was climbing back up to my window. And it wasn't until I managed to scale my way down to the yard that I realized I was also in my pajamas. Without a coat or a sweatshirt or a bathrobe to cover up the cotton shorts and tank I'd slipped on after my shower.

Without my phone.

Fantastic. And how was I supposed to get into my bedroom when I was done? Aunt Julie and Uncle Paul had moved the handy key they used to leave outside for emergencies . . . and hadn't told me where.

Worst Idea Ever? Nice to meet you. Jade Abbott. I'm sure we'll be best friends forever.

Uncle Paul and Aunt Julie's bedroom lights weren't on, Aunt Julie probably having crawled into bed and Uncle Paul probably still at work. If I got caught . . . I didn't want to think about it.

When I was in front of his house, I waited on the sidewalk for a minute, to make sure no one else was at home or awake. I wasn't sure if Quentin had told his parents what happened that night at the bonfire, but either way, me showing up in my jammies and barefoot, looking for their son at night, wouldn't have been the best way to convince them of my innocent intentions.

But no one else floated by the living room window, and no other lights turned on. No one else was here. Hopefully.

Padding up the porch steps, I tried to swallow my heart as I knocked on the front door.

In the background, I could hear something, but I couldn't tell exactly what it was. When I was still standing there a minute later, I knocked again, louder this time.

Footsteps echoed closer, sounding like they were rushing.

When the door burst open, I didn't know who looked more surprised—Quentin or me.

"Jade?" he said, his eyes narrowing like he was trying to make sure it was really me. "What are you doing here?"

My teeth sank into my lip. I thought that would have been obvious, but clearly not. I was working up how to respond to that when a harsh, barking noise rattled from his chest. Or at least from who he was holding against his chest.

"What's the matter with Lily?" I asked, immediately understanding the semi-panicked look on his face.

"I don't know. She's sick. It was only a cough and runny nose this afternoon, but now it's turned into this." Quentin had his phone propped up to his ear; he groaned when voice-mail picked up.

"Where are your parents?" I stepped inside when he started to walk Lily around the living room as she broke into another coughing fit. He was patting her back, bouncing her, soothing her with a shushing noise; if Lily hadn't been so sick, it would have been the sweetest thing I'd ever seen.

"They left with my brothers on an overnight sailing trip. We were going, too, but when Lily started getting sick, I thought it would be better to stay home. So they left. And now I can't get ahold of anyone." Quentin exhaled, pitching his phone at the sofa when another call only ended in another voicemail greeting.

"Okay, okay. Just calm down. It will be all right." I closed the door behind me and started brainstorming. "Babies get sick all the time. It's the way they build up their immune system. She's probably fighting some nasty bug."

Quentin nodded, but his face didn't relax any.

I scanned the room. Everything from a thermometer to stuffed animals to pacifiers were scattered around. From the looks of it, he'd tried everything to soothe her, but obviously nothing had worked. In between the coughing fits, she was crying, giant tears rolling down her cheeks.

"What's her temperature?" I moved closer and ran the back of my hand across her forehead. She felt warm but not scalding.

"Um, let's see." Quentin backed up toward the sofa table, where a piece of paper and a pen were resting. "It was a hundred and one point eight half an hour ago. And I gave her some infant Tylenol an hour ago to help with the fever." When he tried resting Lily in his arms, she really started coughing and crying, so he lifted her upright against his chest again. "I don't know what to do, Jade. I was about to take her to the ER, but I didn't want to go unless it was absolutely necessary, because God only knows how much crud and germs are in a place like that." He backed into the wall behind him, looking totally exhausted. And totally freaked. "I don't know what to do. I *should* know what to do."

Okay, think, Jade. Think.

"High fever. Hard, strange-sounding cough. Wheezing breaths," I listed off, feeling the word on the tip of my tongue. "Croup." I got it out at last. "I think Lily's got croup."

Quentin's forehead creased. "Croup?"

"It's a pretty common virus for young kids and babies to catch. Always comes with that terrible coughing. I think it has something to do with their vocal cords narrowing or something." When Lily started her next coughing fit, it sounded like she was about to bark out her lungs.

Quentin rushed for his phone, but I interrupted him. "Where's the closest bathroom with a shower?"

"What?" he said, still patting Lily's back like he was simultaneously trying to soothe her and knock some of that gunk loose.

"A shower. The hot steam helps relax the vocal cords, making it easier to breathe."

For a moment, he stared at me, like I was speaking a different language.

"Quentin," I said. "Listen to me. Bathroom. Now."

He swallowed, holding my stare while he clung to a screaming, coughing Lily. I'd never seen a person look so vulnerable in my whole life. I wasn't sure I ever would. "Up the stairs. First door on the left."

I jogged up the stairs, hearing him follow behind me. As soon as I stepped into the bathroom, I cranked on the hot water as far as it would go. When Quentin came in, I closed the door behind him and made sure the bathroom window was shut. "She's going to cough a little worse at first, but then it will get better. You have to trust me."

Quentin just nodded, standing there in the middle of the bathroom, watching as the steam started to billow from the shower. When Lily's cough became worse, he had to close his eyes and grit his jaw as he gently bounced her in his arms. It was like someone was driving nails through his toes, one at a time.

"Shh, it's okay, sweetie." I rubbed her little arm flailing all around as she wheezed for air.

It was only a couple of minutes later that Lily's cough started to ease; it felt like hours.

"That's better, isn't it?" I smiled at Lily, who had finally stopped crying and was now looking around the bathroom, not quite sure what she thought of the steam.

Quentin stared at Lily, almost as if he was holding his breath to see if her cough would come back. A look of relief washed over him when she gave a tiny smile and started grabbing at the steam floating above his shoulder.

"Thank God," he breathed, his whole body going kind of limp. Then he turned his head toward me. The skin between his brows was creased and his green eyes didn't sparkle the way I was used to, but still, I felt that look he was giving me in every nerve ending in my body. "Thank *you*."

I shrugged. "Glad I could help."

"How did you know what to do?" he asked. "How did you even know what it was she had?"

I scooted onto the counter beside him. "I told you, official Shrinking Violets babysitter. I've seen pretty much every virus, bacteria, and germ a kid could catch. Croup is especially memorable because of that terrible cough. Sounds like a seal with laryngitis or something."

Half a smile formed on his face. "Sounds exactly like that."

Quentin chuckled softly, watching Lily yawn. "I'm with ya, kid," he said, yawning right after.

"You should get some rest. That cough will probably come back the next few nights. So I'll go, and let you sleep while you can."

"Would you mind staying?" A flash of panic rolled across his face when I started for the door. "I'm sorry, unless you have other plans tonight."

I waved at my pajamas. "Does it look like I do?"

A quiet chuckle rumbled in his chest. "I've taught you nothing."

I smiled, debating. I'd snuck out of the house again, technically while I was grounded and had been expressly told not to even think about it. I was with Quentin, alone, the boy Uncle Paul seemed to be under the impression couldn't wait to impregnate me and run.

If I cared about getting into trouble, I should leave, before I got caught. And I did care about getting into trouble and listening to my aunt, but I cared more about doing what was right. And for whatever reason, I knew staying with Quentin was right.

"You got it," I said, getting comfortable.

Quentin started to nod off when the shower ran out of hot water, but when I turned off the showerhead, he jerked awake, like I'd just blown a trumpet an inch away from his ear.

"What's the matter?" He blinked a few times, instantly awake. Impressive. It was almost like he had lots of experience jerking awake in the middle of the night.

"Nothing. Hot water's out."

His forehead creased as he checked Lily in his arms.

"It's fine. Let's just move outside for a while," I said as calmly as I could. "The cooler night air is good for her cough, too."

Quentin watched a sleeping Lily and swallowed. "Yeah?"

I opened the door and motioned him through it. "Yeah."

He headed for the backyard once we reached the first floor, and I pulled the sliding door open for him. As he padded onto the deck, I snagged a couple of throw blankets from the living room and followed him.

He'd settled onto one of the comfy outdoor couches. I dragged one of the little tables up so he could kick his feet up on it. He looked exhausted now that the adrenaline had stopped pumping.

"You can fall asleep. I can babysit, if you want." I settled down beside him, closer than I'd intended. "I promise I'm capable of taking care of a little person."

He must have caught the slight edge in my voice, because he exhaled, squinting up at the night sky. "Yeah, about that," he started slowly. "I'm sorry. That didn't have anything to do with you. It was me."

"No, it was me. All me. You were right to be upset. My aunt and uncle were right." I shook the blankets out and spread one over Lily, who was snuggled against his chest. "I messed up big-time."

He scoffed. "I don't think I'd call that a big-time mess-up."

I spread the other blanket over Quentin's and my laps and stared up at the sky with him. "You made it seem like that last week." When he didn't say anything, I peeked over at him from the corner of my eye.

"You know how stuff you go through in life makes you, I don't know, extra-sensitive?" he said, swallowing. "How certain issues just get to you more than others?"

"Yeah?"

His shoulder rubbing against mine lifted. "Well, that's mine," he stated. "Not being there when you should be. Bailing on people when they need you."

I nodded like I understood, but I wasn't sure I had a clue. Quentin had both of his parents in his life—neither of them had ditched when he'd been the size of a pinhead in his mom's stomach. But the way he talked about it, I could see how scarred he'd been by the idea of it.

"I'm not usually like that," I said. "I'm normally the total opposite."

"I know that. You're the most responsible person I've ever met—the one I'm trying to make more irresponsible." When he peered over at me, I peeked back. We smiled like we'd been caught. "It's my fault. If you want to point a finger, aim it this way."

I rolled onto my side so I was facing him. "And you're the most responsible person I've ever met who tries really, really hard to pretend he's irresponsible."

He laughed quietly. "Noticed, did you?"

My eyes dropped to where Lily was snoozing soundly on his chest. "Only weeks ago." I tucked the blanket tighter around her. "One responsible person trying to make another responsible person irresponsible is in no way going to be successful."

Even his smile appeared tired. "Can you blame me?" He cocked his brow at me. "You've got the world at your fingertips. I have to live vicariously through you."

My eyes lifted. "What are you talking about? You've got the world at your fingertips, too."

"Funny, it feels more like the world has its fingers around my throat and is slowly squeezing." Quentin raised his hand, curling his fingers around his neck in demonstration.

"I have no idea what you're talking about." I laughed as he played dead with his tongue hanging out for a moment.

His face cleared, and then he was looking at me in that way again. The way that made me feel like I was about to make a bad decision but that it would be one of the best choices I'd ever made. "So maybe I should stop talking," he said in a voice that came from low in his chest.

My stomach fluttered. I wanted to kiss him. So very badly. I knew he was holding something back, but it wasn't like I'd confessed my life story yet, either. Whatever it was, I felt I could trust him. With his secrets. And with mine.

I slid closer. "Maybe you should."

His arm stretched behind me, curving around my neck and gently guiding me toward him. His eyes dropped to my mouth. "Maybe I will."

His head tipped, but right before he kissed me, Quentin paused. His eyes connected with mine, a silent question in them. I answered it.

I touched my lips to his as my hand slid around the side of his neck. And he kissed me back. Like I'd never been kissed before. Like I wasn't sure if I'd ever be kissed again. A kiss was magical no matter who it was with—usually—but this was something else. Something bigger. Something stronger. Something that felt like it was changing me, one touch at a time.

When I twisted to move closer, I ran into an obstacle. Lily. She gave a little baby sigh, but she didn't wake up. Yeah. I'd just had the best kiss of my life with a guy holding his sick baby sister on his chest.

I laughed, but Quentin didn't unwind his arm from around my neck even though we'd stopped kissing. Once I'd caught my breath and shaken the dizziness from my head, I was ready for more. If he could kiss like that, what was I doing wasting time? Why had I wasted so much of this summer when I could have been kissing Quentin and feeling like my lungs were about to explode?

"Wait," he said when I moved in. "I think this is a good time to tell you something. Since we finally just had our first kiss after our third attempt." He was smiling, but his eyes didn't match—they fell more into the freaked realm.

I waited, with his arm around me. I could tell he was wrestling for the right words. I wasn't sure I'd ever seen him struggle so much to say something. From his face, I was bracing myself for the worst.

"Jade, I—" But the opening garage door cut him off. We both twisted our heads when we heard a ruckus coming from inside. "Quentin?!" Mrs. Ford's voice echoed through the house before she rushed out of the sliding door when she saw where we were. "How's Lily? Where is she?" She looked panicked and disheveled and mad with worry. "We finally got your messages. Why weren't you answering your phone?"

"She's here, Mom." Quentin sat up, tucking the blanket down so his mom could see her. "She's fine. Jade knew what to do. She's been here all night." Quentin shot a half smile at me as his mom exhaled a long, shaking breath. "She stayed." Quentin glanced up at his mom. She stroked Lily's head a few times, like she had to make sure she was really here and fine. Then she did the same to Quentin's.

"Good job, sweetie," she said to him. "You did good."

"No. I didn't. I freaked out. I was about ready to strap Silas's strobe light to the top of my truck and blast my horn to get to the ER." Quentin hadn't let go of me when his mom showed up, and now he seemed like he was pulling me closer. "Jade calmed me down and helped Lily. Actually, she helped us both." He beamed at me, like we were the only people on the planet.

But I was very aware of his mom lingering behind us. What she did next, I did not expect.

Mrs. Ford's hand dropped to my shoulder and she patted it softly. "Thank you, Jade." Her voice was tight but strong. "Thank you for being there for them."

Chapter Fifteen

After that night, Quentin and I earned back a little freedom. Especially when I sat down with my aunt and uncle after breakfast and told them the whole story of the previous night. We were figuring our way around each other, one step at a time.

"I really don't like the idea of you walking to the park by yourself, Jade." Aunt Julie fretted again. "Why don't you let me drive you?"

I checked the time on her minivan's dash. "Because you're late meeting Uncle Paul for frozen yogurt." I waved into the backseat, looking for some support from the twins. After I called out Uncle Paul that night about not spending any time getting to know me or his own darn family, he'd been making steady improvements. Less time at work, more time at home—he could even be found sitting at the dinner table with us more nights than not.

"Yeah, Mom. We gotta meet Dad." Hailey unbuckled and waved at the mall where we were parked, where they were meeting Uncle Paul for frozen yogurt.

"I haven't seen Dad all day. I miss him," Hannah added, managing an impressive sad face.

Aunt Julie studied her girls in the rearview mirror, then sighed. "Fine." She unclipped her seat belt. "I'm going to respect the fact that you are a young woman who is used to a hefty amount of freedom and is responsible." Aunt Julie didn't have to say it out loud. Her eyes filled in the rest: *most of the time.*

I already had the door open and was climbing out. "And I'm going to respect the fact that you care about me and are responsible for me by texting once I get to the park, and checking in every hour after that." I showed her my phone so she could see it was on and charged, then started to make my way through the mall parking lot. "Have fun."

The twins were already pulling their mom from the minivan, steering her toward the main mall doors. Who would have thought frozen yogurt could cause such excitement?

It was still light out, and the park was literally only five blocks away, but it felt good to be on my own. Exploring someplace I'd never seen, navigating one block after another. The few times I'd gotten turned around in some of the cities I explored while on tour with my mom, a panicky feeling would settle into my stomach. But I'd always pop out at some local café or great bookstore and realize I wasn't really lost— I was exactly where I was supposed to be at that moment.

I wished that applied to feeling complete as a person, too. Half of me still felt missing because of not knowing my dad. That was why I had to fill in that blank, even if it meant going behind my mom's back.

Her name showed up on my phone. Man, it was like she had telepathy, I swear. I groaned, but knew I had to take the call. I couldn't put this off any longer.

"Mom," I greeted, trying to sound all excited.

"Good. You haven't forgotten who I am. Contrary to the past week's string of missed calls."

I shouldn't have picked up.

"I'm sorry about that. We've both been so busy."

"I'm never too overscheduled to take a call from the person I love most in the world."

I bit the inside of my cheek. "Except when you're in the middle of playing a sold-out concert?"

Mom didn't pause. "I'll give you a code word to say to the stage crew. Say it and I will walk right off that stage, even if I'm in the middle of the chorus to 'Blinders On.'"

I knew she meant it. "I'm sorry. I can talk now. If you can."

"I can talk. If you've got enough minutes left to spend on the woman who gave birth to you. I realize talking on the phone with Quentin Ford for"—the sound of shuffling papers in the background—"five hundred and forty-two minutes *so far* this billing cycle eats up your phone's plan."

Yikes. Had it been that many minutes? Those late-night phone calls really added up. "Wow. Who have you got on intel? Because the White House could probably make better use of your contact." I wiped my forehead because of the hot night, and because this conversation was making me sweat.

"My teenage daughter has just gotten involved in her first serious relationship. I've got more intel on you than the White House could shake a stick at."

Of course she did.

"Listen, Mom, we're taking it slow. Don't worry. He's a good guy. You'd like him."

On the other end, I could hear her huff, as if the only way she could like him was if he moved to another country. "How is spending every night together for the past week taking it slow? My definition is pretty much entirely different."

Great. The sarcasm. Never a good sign.

"I meant we're taking things slow physically," I said, feeling mildly awkward talking about this with Mom. We talked about anything and everything for the most part, but the relationship topic, and how it directly pertained to me, had been left untouched. I'd never had enough time or interest to get serious with the guys I'd met before this.

"So what—you haven't kissed yet?"

My head dropped. So. Awkward. "No, we've kissed." A lot, I added to myself. "But we haven't done anything else."

"Oh, well, that's a relief. Because I'm not quite ready to be a grandmother." And keep the sarcasm rolling. Jeez. Mom was really in a bad mood tonight. It didn't seem like it should have been over me dating a guy, but I knew better. Of all the things in the world, me getting serious when I was too young was the one thing that could get her worked up.

"Mom, come on. I'm not you. I'm not going to get—"

"Pregnant at seventeen by some guy you fell head over heels in love with? Some guy who may not stick around long enough for the stick to turn pink?"

I paused. If for no other reason than to let her know I'd heard her and was giving it thought. I knew she was worried about me. I knew why she was worried. But I wasn't her, and Quentin wasn't my dad. Our situation was totally different.

"I'm not going to get pregnant, Mom. I'm smart. I'm careful. It isn't going to happen." Why did I feel the need to locate some nearby wood I could knock on?

"Just know that if you do, he's going to run, Jade. He's a seventeen-year-old boy. Their definition of responsibility is BYOB."

Anger pulsed in my veins. She wasn't being fair. She didn't know Quentin and hadn't seen him with his family. She didn't have a clue about how responsible he was or wasn't.

"Mom?" I waited a moment before continuing. "I really don't want this to be the first time I ever hang up on you. But I feel like I'm going to if you keep saying that kind of stuff. You're not being fair—you've never even met him." I didn't say it snappy or bitchy, just honestly.

I stopped when I reached the edge of the park, not sure what to say next.

"I love you, Jade. No matter what."

For some reason, this time it sounded different. I think I understood why. "No matter *what* what?" I asked.

Mom sighed, knowing what I was getting at. "My parents turned their backs on me when I told them I was pregnant. At the time, it felt like your aunt did, too. You can tell me anything, whether it is about you approving of censoring music or getting knocked up with triplets—I'll never turn my back on you. *Never.*"

"Thanks, Mom. I love you, too. No matter what."

After we said good-bye, I needed a minute to put myself

back together. At the same time I felt like I was exactly where I belonged, I also felt homesick.

"There you are." Zoey glided down the grassy hill in front of me, her wild hair bouncing as she moved. "I was worried you might have ditched me for your boyfriend."

"Never." I gave her a fake-injured look as she slipped her arm through mine and steered me into the park. I'd loved getting to know and spending time with Zoey. It was so different seeing the same person daily. Her friendship was a serious bonus I hadn't anticipated this summer.

"Where is lover boy, by the way?" she asked.

"Home. Family obligations."

Zoey's nose crinkled. "He's so responsible. It's freaky."

I played with the end of my braid, not sure how to respond to that. Quentin was super-responsible, but I didn't take that as a bad thing, just yeah, unusual. Or "freaky," in Zoey rhetoric.

"I didn't really take you for a farmers market kind of girl," I said instead, taking in the scene up ahead. Mom and I loved farmers markets and had probably spent a life savings on organic produce. However, Zoey leaned more toward the Quentin diet of fried, processed, or preserved when it came to food.

She kept guiding me along, clearly looking for something as we wove through an array of stands and vendors. "What do you mean? I love a farmers market as much as the next girl." She must have found what she'd been looking for, because her face lit up. Her bracelets tinkled when she clapped her hands.

When I saw what she was eyeing, everything made sense. "Kale Boy is kind of cute."

Zoey wasn't blinking, she was so transfixed. "Kale Boy is *divine*."

My hip bumped hers as we kept milling around. "Kale Boy also looks kind of old."

Zoey waved that off like it was trivial. "That might seem like a big deal now, but in five years it won't matter one bit."

"And you're going to wait five years for a guy who peddles bundles of kale for five bucks a pop, drives an old VW van, and clearly has a thing for flannel?" I asked, scanning his setup.

Zoey chewed at her nails, her chipped polish a dark shade of violet today. "Absolutely."

My eyes lifted as she circled a stand that had a selection of cherries and peaches. "Are you going to go over and say hi or something?"

Zoey shook her head. "I prefer to do my pining from a distance."

"That makes no sense."

"It makes a ton of sense. What if he's got this really shrill, high-pitched voice that sounds like he's been sucking on helium? Or what if he has really unfortunate body odor?"

"Other than kale?" I interjected as he heaved another crate of bundles from the back of his van.

"Trust me. It's better to keep my distance and imagine he's perfect in every way possible."

"Nobody's perfect."

Zoey gave me some side-eye. "Quentin Ford seems pretty darn close to it."

We moved on to the next vendor over, who was selling essential oils. "What makes you say that?" I asked, trying to keep it casual and like I wasn't fishing.

"Because it's the truth."

"How do you know? You must know him pretty well to say he's close to perfect."

"Not really." Zoey sniffed a vial of tea-tree oil.

"You guys go to the same school; you work at the same place." I followed her around the booth as she checked out every last oil.

"It's not like we're good friends." After taking a whiff of the key lime, she dug around in her big tote for her wallet. "It's not like he's particularly forthcoming, either. I mean, I've babysat toddlers more willing to share than he."

"You think he's covering something up?"

Zoey dropped her key lime vial into her tote and moved on to the next stand. "Or he's got trust issues, maybe," she mused, sorting through a mason jar of honey sticks. "Doesn't he tell you things?"

My hands slid into my back pockets. "Yeah. He just closes up over some stuff."

"Like what?"

My lips pursed thinking about saying her name. "Blaire."

"I don't know much. Just that she was his old girlfriend at his last school. Lindsey makes it sound like this Blaire chick has a heart made of ice or something, but I don't know any of the details. Want me to see if I can get the scoop from her?"

I chewed on my lip for a moment. Her offer was tempting. "No thanks. I should hear it from him."

"A little mystery's kind of exciting though, right? Like cute Kale Boy—leaves something to the imagination." Zoey gave the kale pusher across the lawn a dreamy stare.

"A little mystery's fine. A whole suspense novel's worth, not so much."

"I'm sure it's no big deal. We're talking about Quentin freaking Ford for crying out loud. He was probably the patron saint of something in his last life."

I pretended to seem interested in the glowing lamps on the table, but my head was totally somewhere else. "I hope you're right."

"Why don't you just ask him? Straight-out. Give him the he-can't-touch-you-until-he-spills ultimatum." Zoey tugged me along to the next vendor. "*Ask* him."

"Okay. I will," I said, conjuring up a smile, like that was so simple.

But it wasn't asking him I was afraid of—it was what his answer would be.

Chapter Sixteen

Suburban life was definitely not as simple and straightforward as I thought it would be. It was every bit as surprising and chaotic as life on the road had been. Just because a person had the same place to come back to each night didn't mean everything else was predictable.

At least that was my experience so far this summer. Right when I thought I had everything under control and had found my groove, life issued me a reality check. For as much time as Quentin and I had been spending together, I still felt something big hanging between us. One minute he'd be sharing some embarrassing moment from puberty, and the next he'd clam up at the slightest mention of his old school and his past.

He was the most open closed-off person I'd ever known.

Boys were confusing. That was the great takeaway of the summer so far.

Crashing on a lounger in Aunt Julie and Uncle Paul's backyard, I pulled up my dad's band's tour page for the tenth time that week. They were still scheduled to play at Mac's

Bar tomorrow night. Tomorrow night, I was going to meet my dad.

Thinking about it made me feel super-anxious. Zoey had sent me a text a few hours ago having to cancel on the concert, so I was flying solo, which made it that much scarier.

"Hey!" I shouted above the shrieks and squeals. "Ten minutes until dinner, so get the sprinkler games out of your system because it's bath time after dinner."

The twins acknowledged me with a wave, while Abe and Silas didn't even seem to hear me. I was on babysitting duty tonight, and this time I hadn't spaced out. When Aunt Julie had asked if I could watch the girls, I was surprised she was giving me a second chance. I was thankful for it, too. So I'd set reminders in my calendar and left random notes in my bedroom, bathroom, and purse so there was no conceivable way I could forget about tonight.

Nothing drastic, but definite changes were happening in the Davenport household. More dinners where Uncle Paul's chair was occupied, time spent playing with his kids, and an evening set aside to take his wife to dinner, like tonight.

"Can Abe and Silas stay?" Hannah hollered, after pirouetting over the sprinkler.

"Sure. If they want to have tofu hot dogs and kale salad."

I don't think I'd ever seen two boys look so grossed out. "No thank you," Abe said, cringing.

"Yeah, they'd rather eat hot dogs made of questionable food content and nitrates. Way more appetizing," Quentin huffed.

Before I could turn around in my lounger, Quentin was stretching into the one beside me. I had the day off, but it looked like he'd come from the pool. He was in his lifeguard shirt and shorts, his sunglasses still in place.

When I stayed quiet, he slid his glasses on top of his head. His eyes gave away how little sleep he'd been getting. They were all dark shadows and bloodshot. We'd gotten into an argument last night when I took Zoey's advice and "just asked him." That didn't go how I'd hoped it would. Instead of answers, I received a whole lot of deflection that escalated into our first fight as an official couple.

"Sorry, Mom asked me to come and get the boys for dinner. I should have given you a warning or something first."

"You don't have to alert me before you come over."

Quentin watched the backyard sprinkler scene for a minute, but it didn't look like he was really seeing it. "I've been thinking a lot about what you said last night."

"I said a lot last night," I said, going through the endless list of things I'd fired at him.

He shifted on his chair, like he couldn't get comfortable. "How you want to do all of these big things with your life. But I can't do them with you."

Ah, *that* thing I'd said last night. Not exactly the topic I was hoping to broach with him. "Why not?"

"Because I'm not that guy," he said, his expression reading that-was-that. "You're looking for some other guy."

"I'm not looking for some other guy. I wasn't even looking for a guy." I motioned at him sitting in the chair. "But you showed up in my life and refused to be ignored." I had to remind myself to keep my voice down, since we weren't exactly alone. "I'm not looking for another guy. I'm happy with the one sitting in front of me."

For the first time, his eyes moved to mine. It was like he was searching for some lie or half-truth in them.

He wasn't going to find one.

"You're leaving at the end of the summer," he said at last.

"So?" I said. He sat up, turning so he was facing me.

"That shouldn't matter," I continued. "You shouldn't willingly give up something great if you don't have to. You shouldn't give it up because of something that might happen. Live in the moment, right? You taught me that." I turned so I was facing him, too, our knees bumping together.

"I'm trying to give you an easy out, Jade." His head fell a little as he studied the patio at his feet.

"I don't want an out."

"My life is complicated."

I didn't disagree, but I wasn't sure I viewed Quentin's life as complicated. Busy, yeah. A slew of responsibilities, sure. But complicated?

"My mom's the lead singer for one of the biggest bands in the world right now. I'm a vegan, a hippie who has never once had a home address." I touched his knee with mine. "I can work around complicated."

He stared at the ground like it was filled with answers he was trying to decode. "Okay. Live in the moment. I can do that." When he looked up at me, he was smiling. "So? What are we doing next?"

With Zoey canceling, I didn't want to go alone to see my dad's band. One, because Mac's Bar looked like a rough place a young girl would not want to walk into by herself, and two, because I guessed I'd need some support, no matter what went down tomorrow night.

I couldn't imagine anyone I'd want at my side more than Quentin.

"There's this band playing tomorrow night." My palms broke out in a cold sweat thinking about it. "You in?"

Quentin's hand capped over my knee as he scooted closer. "I'm in."

I was about to be in the same room as my dad, breathing the same air, for the first time ever. I never knew I'd be such a wreck when this day finally came.

I hadn't been able to eat anything all day, and my hands had been shaking nonstop ever since Quentin picked me up. The rest of my body pretty much felt like it was going to shut down at any moment.

"You doing okay over there?" Quentin asked again after he'd found a spot in the dark parking lot behind Mac's Bar.

I reminded myself to breathe. "I'm doing great. Really," I added when he didn't appear convinced.

"Who's this band we're seeing?" Quentin peered through his windshield, appearing concerned when he inspected the venue. I couldn't blame him, though—it looked like a total dive. Neon signs, half of them burnt out, dozens of patrons in back smoking, and from the lack of windows, it wasn't the kind of place that welcomed light inside.

"Anarchy Artists," I said, swallowing when I started to open the door.

Quentin had already jogged around and was swinging the door open for me, helping me through it and keeping me close as we moved across the parking lot. He kept checking over his shoulder, like someone was about to pounce out of the dark any moment.

"And you listen to this band?" Quentin shot his arm around me when the sound of a beer bottle breaking came close by.

"Yeah. A little." At least a few times, when I forced myself to try to make it through a full song. I was counting on them sounding better in person.

A guy was stationed at the front, but it looked like he was there to break up any fights that started, because he barely checked Quentin's and my IDs. On live-music nights, Mac's let in minors, which was a good thing, since I wasn't sure what my aunt would do if she ever caught me with a fake ID.

"Stay close, okay?" Quentin locked his fingers through mine, then started to push his way into the crowd.

I held on so tightly that my fingers started to ache, but once Quentin had shoved our way to the stage, he let go of my hand long enough to position me in front of him. He braced his arms on either side of me and caged me in. I didn't think I'd be more protected if he'd wound me up in ten layers of bubble wrap.

The bar was dark inside, but the lights dimmed even more when the band started to move on to the stage. If you could call that a stage. It was more a small perch where a set of drums and a couple of guitars could barely fit.

I held my breath as I watched the four musicians take their spots. They all had beers in their hands, which they placed within reach as they got situated. The crowd barely seemed to notice the band was taking the stage. No shouts or hoots or anything. Glancing around, it appeared like I was the only one paying attention.

Even Quentin was watching me more than the stage.

The low lights flickered back on when the first few notes echoed through the bar. The lighting wasn't good. Even when the Shrinking Violets had been the opening act for small bands, their setup was better. Ten times better.

My attention was quickly diverted from the poor lighting to something else, though. The man standing front and center, working his guitar as he kinda staggered up to the mic.

My God. That was him. *My* dad.

I wasn't sure how I'd feel when I saw him, and I wasn't sure I could even explain the way I was feeling right now. It was an odd mix of surprise and relief, shock and disappointment. The music began to play, but I barely noticed it as I scanned my dad's face, searching for physical similarities—the harder I looked, though, the less we appeared to have in common. I'd built him up in my head for so long. The bleary-eyed man practically swaying in front of me, his fingers not able to keep up with the chords, was not the person I'd envisioned.

I reminded myself to be open-minded and fair. This was who my dad was, no matter what I'd imagined.

"Is it me or do they all look drunk?" Quentin had to cup his hand around his mouth and speak right into my ear because it was loud. Screeching, shrieking, acoustics-suck loud.

"They're probably tired from touring. It's exhausting with all of the travel and performing." I didn't mean to sound defensive, but from the look Quentin gave me, I knew I did.

"What kind of a tour have these guys been on?" He cringed when the lead singer, aka Dad, hit a particularly bad note. "The retirement-home scene? I'm sure they're huge with people who are hard of hearing and seeing."

I bit my tongue to keep from saying anything I'd regret. Quentin was right—they were bad—but this was my dad's band. I couldn't laugh and joke with him about how terrible they were. What kind of daughter would that make me?

When he didn't get the reaction out of me he was expecting, he stayed quiet. No more jokes, no more pretending his ears were bleeding; he stayed silent and still beside me, shoving the occasional jerk who stumbled into us.

I knew what he was thinking when we were still standing there as the band struggled to get their eighth and final song out. He was wondering what we were doing here. I didn't blame him.

When Anarchy Artists finished their set, no one applauded. No one called for an encore. The crowd barely acknowledged that there'd been live music at all. I might have clapped to at least show some appreciation, but I was too shocked to move.

My mom and her band were the real deal. They always had been, even before they finally got noticed and picked up by a big label. Music was their passion, the way writing was mine.

Anarchy Artists, with their drunken fumbling, clearly had no passion. Well, except for one thing.

As the band came offstage, I noticed a few girls started to circle around them, touching and talking, giggling and grinding. The bartender made sure they had fresh drinks in their hands, too. So, booze. And women. God, maybe his social media posts had been an accurate depiction of who he was.

"Ready to go?" Quentin asked, slowly steering me away from the stage toward the exit.

Maybe I should have gone. Maybe I should have been content to keep my dad in the box I'd kept him in for a while now, happy to imagine he was whoever I wanted him to be— the Kale Boy of dads.

But I'd come so far. Worked so hard to get to this moment, going behind my mom's back and investing hundreds of hours cyberstalking him. I couldn't walk away. I couldn't do the same thing he'd done to her, because what if he'd been wondering about me, too? What if he'd been trying to find me?

He'd walked away years ago. But I couldn't.

"Wait." I pulled away from Quentin and headed toward the bar.

Quentin closed in behind me instantly, shielding me from a big guy who'd staggered, spilling his drink all over Quentin's back instead of down my front. He didn't even flinch, but I did. "Sorry," I said, peeking behind to see how drenched he'd gotten. Of course the guy's cup had been full.

"Trust me. Coming out of here smelling like beer is the least of my worries." Quentin's eyes flickered up to where the band was perched on stools, entertaining their admirers. The jig was up. Quentin knew I was here for a reason—other than wanting to listen to live music.

"Are you going to tell me what's going on now, Jade?" Quentin's hand came around my arm, but he didn't stop me. He let me keep going, moving with me. "Why we're here?"

I was a few steps away from my dad. I should have been feeling something, right? Something other than uncertainty? This person had given me half of my DNA, and all the emotion I could conjure up was doubt, mixed with a bit of resolve?

"That's my dad," I said, swallowing. "And I'm finally about to meet him."

Quentin broke to a stop the moment he heard me say *dad*. Even though he snapped out of it quickly, it wasn't fast enough to pull me back before I'd shoved my way up to the groupie herd.

At first he didn't notice me. He was too busy "watching" the girl who'd pretty much plopped herself directly in his lap. It wasn't until I cleared my throat and said his name—his real name—that I got his attention. At least some of it.

"Robbie Devine."

He kind of gawked at me, taking me in standing there in front of him, a seventeen-year-old girl in a sea of half-naked women. "Who the hell are you?" he asked, still grinning at me like I was providing free entertainment.

By then Quentin had come up behind me, shoving his way into the circle. "Let's get out of here, Jade," he whispered, trying to steer me away. "You don't want to do this."

I shook him off, lifting my shoulders and trying to look "Dad" in the eye. "Hi. Robert Devine, right? I'm Jade Abbott, your daughter."

At first there was silence. A few shocked faces and a few disbelieving ones, but there was only one face I was watching. My dad's stayed frozen in that same amused way for a moment, and then his mouth fell open and he started to chuckle. Like this was one big joke.

I felt Quentin start to move around me, his body tense. Suddenly it felt like Quentin wasn't trying to pull me away anymore but trying to hold himself back.

"It's true. I *am* your daughter." When a few others joined in the laughter, I blurted out, "Meg Abbott's my mom. You two were together when you were both seventeen and she got pregnant. You walked away, but she had me, and now I'm here." Not sure what else to say. I'd told him. I'd given him the details. What happened next was up to him.

"Kid, I don't have a clue who Meg Abbott even is. I wasn't exactly an exclusive kind of guy when it came to relationships back then." His arm wound tighter around the girl still sitting on his lap. "I'm not exactly an exclusive type of guy now. Maybe I did get it on with your mom, maybe I didn't." His shoulders lifted in the most dismissive way possible. "But if I were to take the word of every kid who's ever marched up to me proclaiming I'm their dad, I'd owe millions in child support." He shook his head, chuckling again, like I hadn't just poured myself into this moment. Like I hadn't invested time and energy and heartache to get here, looking this man in the eye and telling him who I was.

And what was his reaction? A chuckle and a shrug.

"Now get out of here, kid. Even if I am your dad, I'm not the fatherly type." Nudging one of his bandmates, he turned around in his stool, pulling another girl onto his lap with the other arm. He'd turned his back to me and was essentially walking away. It wasn't only my mom he'd left that day; it was me, too. I'd been too blind or stupid to realize that. I thought it had something to do with her or them, not me. But no, it had to do with me. It probably had everything to do with me.

It was too much. This was not the man I'd envisioned. Not the dad I'd hoped for. I hadn't realized how much this moment would mean to me until it blew up in my face.

When I staggered back, Quentin was there to catch me. He wound his arms around me, wrapped me close, and whispered soothing things into my ear. My whole world felt like it was collapsing, but Quentin was there to hold it all together.

It should have been my dad, but it wasn't. I'd been born into the life I had, and I could either make the best of it or make the worst of it. We didn't all get a choice in what life handed us, but we still had to move forward. We didn't get to choose our parents, but we got to choose our friends.

I couldn't imagine choosing a better one than Quentin.

"Ready to get out of here?" he asked, rubbing my back.

All I could do was nod, because I was crying too hard to talk. Part of me was waiting for my dad to call my name before I could get to the door. I was waiting for him to come running after me as I headed into the parking lot. I was still holding on to the hope that that wasn't really who he was, but when Quentin opened his truck door for me and I crawled inside, I accepted that my dad wasn't coming after me. He didn't care. He'd already forgotten about me. Again.

Accepting that brought on a fresh stream of tears, so I dropped my head into my hands and let myself cry. I knew Quentin was right beside me, witnessing it all, but I didn't care. I'd just had my soul crushed; there was nothing left to bare to him.

"Wait here a minute." Quentin tucked my legs inside, making sure my skirt was all the way in. "I'll be right back." There was no mistaking the anger in his voice as he closed the door behind him, the sound of his footsteps as he jogged along the gravel lot.

He wasn't gone long. Maybe two or three minutes, but by the time he returned I'd managed to cry myself out. My body was still shaking, but no more tears would come. I was bone dry.

Quentin was shaking one of his fists. The knuckles on it were red and puffy-looking.

"What happened?" I asked, wiping at my eyes so I could see better.

"Exactly what needed to happen." He still sounded angry, and his expression mirrored that.

"What did you do to him?" I asked.

"Nothing he didn't deserve," he answered, flexing his fingers like he was trying to work sensation back into them.

I rubbed at my face, sniffling and trying to get myself under control. "Tell me you didn't march back in there and punch him?" I already knew the answer, but asked just on the off chance I was wrong.

"Oh, I punched him, all right." Quentin's red fist curled around the steering wheel. "Right before I told him he'd just turned his back on one of the best things that would ever happen to him."

I'd fallen apart. I knew that. But those words were the start of putting myself back together. "Maybe he's got more best things in his life than he can count. How can you be so sure that I'd be one of them?"

Quentin's hand reached for mine. "Because you're one of the best things that could happen to anyone." After he started his truck, he sat there, keeping it in park.

"Listen, Jade," he exhaled, rubbing his forehead. "I've got something I need to tell you. Something important. After tonight . . . I can't put it off any longer."

My eyebrows pulled together as I watched him. Everything about the boy sitting beside me appeared to exude light—what secret did he have that was so dark it crippled him whenever he hinted at it? I couldn't imagine it was half as bad as he made it out to be.

"We both work tomorrow," he continued. "Are you free tomorrow night?"

I shrugged. I'd been free every night this summer. "Yeah."

"Okay. Good." His expression was a mix of relief and terror.

"Quentin? Just so you know, there's nothing you could tell me that would scare me off." My hand gave a gentle squeeze. "I don't scare easily."

He smiled.

Then his fingers curled into mine. "I know you don't."

Chapter Seventeen

The morning after discovering your dad is quite possibly the king of the losers is one you don't want to get up early for.

After dropping me off last night, Quentin asked if I wanted him to stay and talk or anything. It was a nice offer, but I didn't think there was any amount of talking that would make it easier to accept that my dad was not a "dad type" at all. It was more a matter of letting my head wrap around that reality slowly. Besides, from the sound of it, we'd have plenty to talk about tonight. . . .

My shift was dragging today and I wasn't in the best of moods, so that made the day that much worse. I'd forced myself into a corner to count to ten, after snapping at some kid for asking for extra ketchup on his hot dog, when my phone vibrated in my pocket.

Maybe it was someone letting me know I'd been punked and that the whole disaster that was last night had been a huge joke.

Or not.

It was a text from my mom. A longer one than usual, but it took me a while to read it because my eyes started to blur after the first few words. I hadn't told her about last night. I wasn't sure if I ever would. But it was like she'd known. Or at least had a premonition I'd needed to hear from her.

I love you no matter what. Followed by: *But I also love you because you're the best, most wonderful person ever. And no, I'm not biased. Just honest.*

I read her message a few more times, rubbing at my eyes in between reads so they didn't start flooding again. I felt better instantly; knowing that I'd seriously scored in one parent department almost made up for pulling the short stick in the other.

After getting myself back together, I headed to the counter to take the next order. I couldn't help being distracted by the girls who were next in line. I distantly recognized one of them but couldn't place her. I definitely recognized the other one and wanted to put her in her place.

I hadn't seen Ashlyn the past few days—she hadn't been loitering at the pool like usual. I'd hoped it was because she'd moved on and found some other person to torment. So much for that idea.

I sucked in a breath and prepared myself for battle.

"Hi," I greeted the other girl, doing my best to ignore Ashlyn. "What can I get you?"

"I'll have a firecracker, please." The girl smiled at me, like she was trying to place me, too.

"And I'll take a double scoop of crisis averted," Ashlyn said. Her voice made me cringe. Literally. It wasn't a pleasant timbre.

"Here's your firecracker." I handed over the plastic-wrapped popsicle, ringing it up.

"This is Lindsey. In case you forgot." Ashlyn scooted up closer to the counter. "You two met at the bonfire." She smirked when I frowned at the memory.

"Oh, yeah. How could I forget someone I met twice? You and Quentin used to go to school together, right?" I played it cool, taking her money and making change.

Lindsey nodded. "Good memory."

"Lindsey and I are friends with Blaire."

There was that name again.

"Blaire?"

One side of Ashlyn's mouth lifted. "I'm sure you know all about her already. Quentin's probably told you everything. Being such an open and honest guy and all."

I guessed there was a point to all this, but I wasn't going to waste my time trying to figure it out. "Nice to see you again, Lindsey. See you around." I scooted down the counter, trying to take the next order.

"Do you like stories, Jade?" Ashlyn scooted with me. "We have a really good one about Quentin."

My heart stopped as I silently wished Zoey was there to save me, but I did my best to keep my cool. "Sometimes?"

"Well, I bet you already know all about Quentin. With you two being so tight now."

I didn't miss the confused look Lindsey shot Ashlyn, like she also wanted to know where this crazy train was going.

"Whatever, Ashlyn."

"I've got to hand it to you, you're a bigger person than me. There's no way I could deal with that whole mess. No. Way."

She clucked her tongue, seeming to hang on my every move. She was baiting me. Big-time.

I wasn't going to bite.

I fought back a dozen comebacks trying to ignore her and finally managed to catch the next order. Two triple scoops. I'd never been so thankful for the distraction of ice cream.

"I've known some guys with baggage, but yikes." Ashlyn kept going, rolling her nails across the counter. "A one-year-old and no baby mama around?" She paused, letting that settle in the air. "You can have him. He's all yours."

My hand froze, the rest of my body following. *Ignore her. Ignore her. Ignore her.*

"What are you talking about?"

Fail.

From her triumphant smile at seeing my surprise, I knew I'd confirmed something for her. I'd taken the bait.

Ashlyn lifted her hand. "Ya know. His daughter."

The ice cream scoop fell from my hand. When my head whipped in Lindsey's direction, the look on her face told me everything. Ashlyn was beaming with glee, while Lindsey was burning with regret.

"Oh my God! I thought you knew. I thought Quentin would have told you." Lindsey dragged her sunglasses down over her eyes, shaking her head. "I'm so sorry."

Ashlyn hung her arm around Lindsey's shoulders. "You didn't know? He really didn't tell you he had a kid?" Ashlyn faked shock and awe, blinking at me. "Guess he was too busy working on making another baby with you to mention the one he was already raising, right?"

My arms curled around my stomach.

This *wasn't* happening. It couldn't be.

"Lily?" I asked. Now Lindsey looked like a deer caught in headlights.

She let out a breath, then nodded. "Yeah. It's Lily."

I didn't know I'd been falling back until I rammed into the counter behind me.

"You don't look so good. You might be coming down with something." Ashlyn's concern came in the form of a twisted smile. "Or you could be knocked up, I guess. But on the bright side, at least you know the dad will hang around to change diapers and shit. You could have done worse."

Lindsey hissed something at Ashlyn. You could tell she wanted her to shut her trap, but Ashlyn didn't appear the slightest bit concerned.

Everything was spinning. Or else I was. I felt like someone had stuck me on a carousel and punched it into hyperdrive. I needed to get out of here. Now.

I could tell Zoey was taking over the shift as she clocked in at the office, so I bolted.

Lily was Quentin's daughter. How was that even *possible*? How had I not seen it? Why hadn't he told me?

Now everything started to make sense. His family moving, all of his talk about "responsibilities," his choice to stay close to home for college. Saying he wasn't the guy I was looking for, his "complicated life" comments.

Well, if Quentin thought his life was so complicated that he needed to keep secrets, I knew one way to simplify it for him: take myself out.

I waved to Zoey, motioning that I was leaving. She gave

me a weird look, mouthing *Are you okay?* I didn't answer. I kept going. I couldn't move fast enough. I was hoping that the faster I moved, the quicker I could put this all behind me.

Right as I turned the corner of the exit to the pool, I crashed into someone.

"Wow. Sorry. You okay?" It took us both a moment to realize who we'd crashed into.

He was showing up for his shift. He was happy to see me. He didn't have a clue about what I'd just learned.

It made my throat burn. It made everything burn. How could someone look at me like that and keep this massive, giant secret from me?

"What's the matter, Jade?" He'd noticed the look on my face. "Is this about your dad? Do you want to talk about it? I've only got a few minutes before my shift starts, but I'm sure someone could cover me for a while."

My blood was rolling to a boil. I could feel it. At the same time I felt hurt, I was also angry. Actually, those two words didn't come close to describing how I was feeling right now.

"This isn't about my dad." I didn't recognize my voice as I shoved away from his hold. I didn't want him to touch me. I didn't want him to ever touch me again. "This is about *you*." When my eyes lifted to his, I think he saw it. I think he knew that I knew. "*You're* a dad." I didn't say anything else, I just shoved past him and kept going.

"Shit. Jade. Wait." When his hand grabbed mine, I whipped around, firing a warning glare at him.

"Don't touch me," I seethed, still backing away. "Don't talk to me. Don't come close to me ever again."

Quentin stayed where he was, his face twisting into an expression I'd never seen there before. "I was going to tell you."

"Well, now you can save yourself the hassle. Because I already know."

He looked like he was fighting moving closer, but he took a step toward me. "I didn't want to tell you until I knew for sure."

"Until you knew for sure what? That I was good and invested?" I wiped at my eyes, not wanting to cry in front of him. I'd done enough of that last night, and I didn't want him to know that this betrayal had been as painful, if not more so, as my dad's.

He took a breath. As he let it out, his eyes claimed mine. "Until I knew I loved you."

My body froze. My heart already had. "You don't love me, Quentin. Because if that were true, *you* would have told me about Lily. Not someone else."

He looked at a loss for words. He looked at a loss for a lot more. "Jade . . . ," he managed as I found my step.

"I don't ever want to see you again." I spun around and started running. What followed after that was a blur. Mostly. I remembered climbing on Lemon and pedaling as fast as my legs could go. Swiping at my eyes, angry at the tears I was shedding yet again over some guy who'd totally failed me. And dropping Lemon in the yard and flying through the front door of my aunt and uncle's house, barreling up the stairs, and locking myself in my room.

Uncle Paul was at work and Aunt Julie and the girls were at a violin day camp, so I knew I could scream as loudly as I wanted and no one would hear. I could stomp and shout until I felt better, but I also knew nothing would help. Not this time. First my dad.

And now Quentin.

My whole plan for the summer had gone to crap. So much for a normal, everyday summer.

What was I going to do?

My phone rang, like it was somehow answering my question. When I saw who was calling, I had my answer.

"Mom?" I hadn't meant to sound so pathetic, but I wasn't sure I was capable of anything else.

"Oh, baby. What's wrong?" Hearing her voice—the concerned soft one—made me feel impossibly homesick. I missed my mom and being on the road. I missed my old life. As quirky and unscheduled as it had been, it had never been as chaotic and unpredictable as this summer turned out to be.

"Everything." I started to sob again. Choking, rocking wails.

"Jade, talk to me. You're scaring me." Mom was trying to stay calm, but I could hear her voice tremble. "Is this about that boy? Quentin?"

Hearing his name made my back shake with a fresh sob. "How pathetic am I, right? That I'm losing it over some boy I practically just met?" Mom was the torchbearer of the boys-aren't-worth-it philosophy, and her own daughter was acting like the world was over because of one.

"You're not pathetic, sweetie. It's not pathetic to care for another person."

Her voice was exactly what I needed. But I needed something else, too. To leave this disaster behind. Rising, I marched toward the closet, threw my suitcase onto the bed, and unzipped it. The sooner I got out of here, the better I'd feel.

"What happened?" she repeated. "What did he do?"

I dropped the first load of clothes from the dresser into my suitcase. "He lied."

"About what?"

Images of him and Lily flashed through my head. Images of him making faces at her, holding her to his chest, losing his mind when she was sick . . . I needed to set a match to all of them.

"About being a dad."

That finally shut Mom up.

"*What?*" she said a minute later, sounding confused.

"He has a daughter." I had to take a breath to keep from choking on another sob. "Lily's his daughter."

Another stretch of silence, though not as long as the first. "The baby you helped him with when she was sick? That's his *daughter?*"

I nodded manically as I dumped another load of clothes into the suitcase. I didn't care about wrinkles or efficient packing—I just needed out of this nightmare.

"His *daughter,* not his sister." I was an idiot. Why hadn't I seen it? The signs were so obvious now that I knew.

"Did he tell you she was his sister?"

I was about to answer her question, when I stalled. I flipped through the memory banks, and then again, but I couldn't recall a single time where he'd called Lily his sister.

"He lied by omission."

"That doesn't make it a lie. That makes it a secret."

I slammed one dresser drawer closed and tore open the next. "Whose side are you on here, Mom?" Unbelievable. Meg Abbott was defending the teenage boy with a baby.

"Yours. Always yours, Jade." She waited, like she was daring me to challenge her on that again. "But I'm trying to talk you through this because I know a little something about being a young parent and not exactly wanting to advertise it to everyone I came in contact with. It's hard enough without having to deal with everyone being a judgy prick."

When I saw my face in the mirror, I barely recognized myself. I was a wreck. A red, puffy, disheveled hot mess. "I'm not someone he 'came in contact with.' I'm the person he spent the past two months with. That's someone you're supposed to tell if you have any offspring."

Mom exhaled. I could imagine the way she was rubbing at her temples. "I'm not defending him, baby. I'm trying to shed a little light on the situation. He has a child. And it sounds like he was trying to do what was best for her first and foremost. Like I did with you." She paused to take a breath, while I kept cleaning out drawers until all I had left was the closet. "Have you given him a chance to explain why he didn't tell you?"

"What's there to explain?"

"His reasons for why he kept it from you."

"Because he's a selfish jerk who wanted to have a summer fling with some girl he thought was either too naive or too stupid to figure out the truth?"

"He chose to raise his daughter as a single parent. He's not the selfish type, sweetie."

My head was hurting. Either from all the crying or from

all the sense my mom was trying to make out of it. As much as I wanted to tell her she was crazy, I knew she wasn't.

"Mom, please, I need to leave. Today. Right *now*." When I went to try to zip the suitcase closed, I realized my packing style of tossing things wasn't working out so well. "I can't talk about Quentin right now. I need to leave."

Mom was quiet for so long, I checked my phone to make sure I hadn't lost the connection.

"You're throwing in the towel? You're over the quest for a normal summer?"

I sat down on top of the suitcase. "So over it. This whole idea was a bad one. Worst ever. I want to spend what's left of summer with you and the band. Where are you?"

More silence. "We just landed in Vancouver. We'll be here for the next couple of days. But, Jade—"

"I'm heading to the airport. I'm on the first plane I can get on."

"Wait. No. Have you talked to your aunt and uncle about this yet? Do they know what's going on?" She must have taken my silence as an answer. "You need to tell them what happened and what your plan is first, Jade. You can't run away like that without so much as an explanation. That's not how we deal with our problems." There was an edge in her voice, one that suggested it wasn't only my situation she was talking about.

"I need out of here. Right. Now." The long side of the suitcase was zipped—one more side to go and I was free once I'd shoved what was left into my duffel.

"After you talk to your aunt and uncle," she warned. "That will give me time to get you a ticket booked, too."

I was fighting with the last part of the zipper, praying it wouldn't bust.

"Jade?"

The zipper made it, finally. "Yeah, Mom. I heard ya."

"Good. Let me know once you've talked to Julie and Paul, and then I'll let you know what flight you're on."

I made a noise that sounded like I was confirming her plan, but it was more of a grunt of acknowledgment, not agreement.

"Love you, baby. You're a strong person. You'll recover from this, I promise."

"I don't feel strong right now," I whispered, stuffing my duffel with all of my toiletries from the bathroom.

"Strength isn't about never being weak. Strength is about keeping going when you'd rather curl up into a ball and wither away." She was quiet a moment, then added, "I'll see you soon."

The line went dead, but I kept the phone tucked to my ear. It was almost like I could still hear my mom's voice on the other end, reassuring me, comforting me. She would see me soon.

Chapter Eighteen

The whole ride to the airport, I kept staring at my phone. When I realized whose name I was hoping would flash on my screen, I tucked it back into my pocket.

I didn't want to hear from him again in this life or the next one.

I'd left a note for Aunt Julie so she wouldn't freak when she got home and found me and my suitcase gone. She'd probably still lose it, but at least she'd know I was safe and had a plan.

I got off at the first terminal the bus stopped at. I didn't know which airline had the quickest flight to Vancouver, but I was going to find it. Thanks to Mom's shiny credit card, I had a one-way ticket in less than five minutes, my suitcase checked and ready to meet me in another country.

When I made it to the security checkpoint, ticket and passport in hand, I froze up. I wasn't sure why. Other than boarding the plane, this was the last step to get out of here. Go through those gates and that body-scanning machine thing and I was as good as free. Only, I didn't feel like that. The closer I moved toward the security checkpoint, the heavier I felt. Almost like someone was balancing cinder blocks on my head, one for every step I took.

I was running away.

Leaving.

Escaping.

Turning my back and walking away when life got hard and I didn't want to deal.

Suddenly I backed up until I reached a row of plastic chairs lined up against a wall. Running away from my problems. Leaving when the going got tough. I knew it wasn't like I was my dad and leaving behind my unborn child or anything, but I didn't want to feel like a quitter, too.

Dropping my duffel at my feet, I let my head fall into my hands and started crying. I'd been betrayed by two dads in two different ways. One by leaving, and one by lying.

My flight still wasn't for another few hours, but I wasn't sure if I could make it through those security gates even if I had more time. Everything inside me felt dead.

I don't know how long I'd been sitting there, lost and reeling, when I heard someone approach me. It didn't take long for me to recognize the sneakers that had just stepped into the patch of tile I was staring at.

"If you meant what you said about never wanting to see me again, you might not want to look up for the next few minutes. Or however long it takes me to say what I need to."

"How did you find me?"

"It was pretty easy to guess where you'd go after what happened this afternoon. Then I just had to check the Shrinking Violets' tour schedule to see which city you'd be heading to on the first flight out."

My body shifted. He'd only known me a couple of months and knew what I'd do when life got too overwhelming.

"Go away, Quentin. Please." My fingers combed my hair as I closed my eyes.

"We agreed to get together tonight so I could tell you something important. And the airport works just fine for me."

I wanted to cover my ears. I wished I was through security already.

"Lily's mine. She's my daughter." He exhaled heavily, as if a massive weight had fallen off him. "Her mom didn't want her from the very second she found out she was pregnant, but I managed to convince her to have the baby. I've been raising Lily on my own with help from my parents. I don't think I could have survived the past year without them."

He paused to clear his throat. Mine felt like it was being ripped into pieces. "We moved because after Lily was born, no one acted the same around me, you know? No one treated us the same. People either ignored us altogether or pitied us. It was nice having a new place to start over, a clean slate."

My eyes opened, and I found his sneakers had shuffled closer.

"We didn't tell anyone about Lily being mine. The neighbors, the students at my new school, the people I work with at the pool. Everyone assumed she was my sister, and we didn't correct them."

"Yeah." My voice was raspy from the long stretch of silence. "That part of the story I'm familiar with."

"I was going to tell you, Jade."

I said nothing.

Quentin sighed. "I should have told you sooner. Hindsight's a bitch, but if I could go back and do it again, I would have told you first thing."

My back rose when I huffed.

"My family sacrificed their lives for me. Lily's life is dependent on mine." His voice grew louder. "I couldn't ignore all that and tell some girl I'd just met—some girl who was taking off once summer was over."

"Well, *some girl* understands everything now. So thank you for the explanation, carry on, have a nice life." I waved my hand, hoping he'd leave.

"Damn it, stop twisting my words around, Jade. You're not *some girl* to me. You're *the girl,* but there's someone else in my life I have to think about, too. Someone I have to put first, always."

"This wasn't just about you putting your daughter's interests first, Quentin." I leveled him with a glare that made him fall back a step. "This was about you putting your interests first, too."

Quentin collapsed into the chair beside me. "Yeah, that was part of it. I liked you, Jade. A lot. A whole lot more than I was expecting to and a hell of a lot more than I should have, given my situation." He clasped his hands together as he leaned forward in his seat. "You are so free to be and do whatever you want. You see differently than anyone else. You're tough one moment and sweet the next. I wasn't expecting to have the feelings I have for you. If I had, I would have left you alone."

When I lifted my eyebrow, he sighed. "Or maybe I wouldn't have." He paused, chewing on the inside of his cheek. "I loved how I felt when I was with you. I loved feeling like I was any other guy who felt as though anything was possible. I liked just getting to be me when I was with you. The old me. I knew that telling you about Lily might push you away, and I already knew you were leaving at the end of summer—"

"So you thought you could keep your daughter a secret from me and I'd never find out? And this was okay with you?" My words cut sharper than I'd intended, but I wasn't sure if this was making everything easier to understand or harder.

"No. Shit. None of this is okay with me." He popped out of his chair suddenly. "It's not okay that you found out the way you did. It's not okay I waited so long to tell you. It's not okay I let myself fall for you in the first place." He sucked in a deep breath. "It's not okay Lily has some dad who's barely making it, and it's not okay she has a mom who doesn't want anything to do with her." He smacked his palm against the wall. "You both deserve the best. And instead, you both wound up with me."

My throat bobbed. "Blaire? Your old girlfriend from your other school?"

He nodded. "Her parents took her out of school when she started to show and had her tutored at home. Ashlyn and Lindsey were the only other ones who knew about it."

"Did you love her?"

He shook his head. "No. But I love what we made together. Lily. I love my daughter. I love her so much I wouldn't change anything if I could go back and do it again. Not even knowing how hard it was and is and probably always will be. I wouldn't change any of it, Jade."

My back trembled. "There were times before? When you tried telling me, didn't you?"

His hands slid into his pockets. "Yeah, a couple times I tried. Not that it really counts, since I never actually did."

I didn't feel the tear until it splattered on my wrist. "Thank you," I said. "Thank you for telling me your version of it."

"I owed you an explanation tonight. I'm sorry someone beat me to it."

I bit my lip. "Me too."

Quentin shoved off the wall and bent toward me. I couldn't look up at him. It wasn't because I was angry but because I was starting to realize how much I felt for him.

"I know this might sound weird, but I have to say it." He slid his hands into his pockets, shifting. "If Lily turns out to be half the person you are, as a dad I'll be damn proud." He turned to leave. "Have a happy life, Jade. And don't settle for anything or anyone. You deserve better. So don't settle."

All I could do was keep biting my lip and nodding as he walked away. I could have said a hundred things back, there were a million things running through my mind, but I let him walk away. I let him go, because I didn't see any path for us other than the one we'd already been on, and I knew we could never find our way back.

I started crying again.

Quentin was gone.

He'd said I was someone a dad would be proud of.

He had a daughter.

And holy crap, I hadn't let the pool know I was leaving.

Everything was piling on me, until I was buried.

How was I going to crawl out from underneath this and heal alone?

"As your parent, I feel like I should ground you until you're sixty. But as your mom, I kind of just want to give you a big hug."

When I looked up, I blinked a few times to make sure I was seeing right. "Mom?" I glanced up and down the terminal, trying to figure out where she'd come from. "What are you doing *here*?"

"That's the same question I should be asking *you*." Her hand settled on her hip as she looked down at me, but the next moment she held her arms open and pulled me in.

I pretty much leaped out of that chair.

"Whoa." A puff of air burst from her. "I missed you, too, baby."

My arms cinched so tightly around her they started to shake a little. I didn't realize I'd missed every little piece of her, from the sandalwood essential oil she dabbed on her pulse points to the way her hair felt, brushing across my face when she hugged me. I'd missed it all.

"How did you get here so quickly?" My voice was muffled against her worn leather jacket.

"The really great thing about making it big is that all of these credit card companies send you these shiny black cards with no limits. Makes chartering a last-minute plane into Burbank really easy."

Mom kissed my temple and smiled down at me. "So tell me: What are you doing here? And I'm willing to bet that shiny black card that you have not talked with your aunt and uncle about this whole leaving thing."

My head dropped onto her shoulder. I felt instantly better now that she was here. "I didn't talk to them. I left a note." Mom grumbled something about not another note. "I couldn't hang around waiting. I had to get away—out of there and away from everything."

"Looks like you didn't take the final step." Mom pointed at the buzzing security area.

"Yeah, I was having trouble with that last little bit. Kind of felt paralyzed."

"That's because you've got a conscience, oh daughter of mine, and you know that running away from a problem is never a way to deal with it. Head down that path and you'll never stop running."

She didn't have to say it for me to know who she was talking about. "I saw him," I started slowly. "I met my dad."

Mom's hands rubbing my back stopped. "When?" Her voice was too controlled, too casual-sounding.

"Last night," I admitted.

Her body seemed to go rigid all at once, before relaxing a moment later. Her hands started rubbing circles into my back again. "Well, you have had quite the twenty-four hours, haven't you?"

"I don't even want to think about it."

Mom twisted my hair up in her hand like she'd been doing as long as I could remember. "How did it go? With your dad?"

I shook my head. "I bet you can guess."

"I'm sure I can," she whispered. "This was why you wanted to spend the summer with your aunt and uncle, right? Because you wanted to meet him and thought I wouldn't let you?"

I nodded.

"Oh, Jade, it wasn't that I didn't want you to meet your dad. It was never that."

"You just wished I had a different dad?" I guessed, glancing up at her.

She shook her head. "Not a different dad, but maybe that the one you had wasn't such a . . ."

"Loser?" I suggested.

Mom tipped her head left and right, like she was hoping another option would present itself. "Pretty much, yeah."

I started smiling. When Mom saw it, she started to smile, too. "Oh, babe, I'm sorry your dad didn't get a chance to see how amazing you are. But it's only because he doesn't know the first thing about amazing. He doesn't even know it exists, and he wouldn't recognize it if amazing started growing on his"—she cut herself short—"on his forehead. It has nothing to do with you, Jade. Trust me. It's him."

Mom was such an awesome person. I knew it wasn't cool to think your mom was great, but she was. She cared about others and had this amazing laugh and worked so hard. How could he have walked away from her after he found out she was pregnant? How could he just leave like that?

"How do you not hate him?" I asked her.

One of the only tears I'd ever seen come from my mom fell down her cheek. She held her smile. "Because if it wasn't for him, I wouldn't have you."

I checked the time on the wall across from us. My flight wasn't for a few hours, but I wasn't going to be on board.

I'd never been so thankful to miss a flight, because I didn't want to start down a dangerous path. I didn't want to be like my dad, bailing when things got tough. No, I wanted to be like my mom, who dug in her heels, rolled up her sleeves, and chased life when it got hard.

I wanted to be like Quentin, who hadn't turned his back on his baby girl like my dad had with me. Because if you ran from every problem that came at you, you might never get to discover the miracle hiding behind it.

"So? Who are you most upset with? Quentin? Or your dad?" Mom asked gently, waiting patiently for my answer.

"My dad." I bit my lip. "But I'm angry at Quentin, too."

Mom nodded, her long earrings tinkling against her shoulders. "Are you angry at him because he has a child, or because he didn't tell you about having a child?"

"Because he didn't tell me," I answered immediately. It wasn't Lily. It wasn't that he was a teenage dad. Yeah, it wasn't your everyday, but it wasn't something I'd list in the deal-breaker part of a relationship column.

"Is this something you're willing to let him try to explain? Or is it just over, no matter what he has to say?" Mom asked, scooting to the edge of her chair. "Because I am on your side always, but as a former teen parent, I have some useful insight into the mind of another one. I imagine he didn't tell you about his daughter not to hurt you, but to protect her. To protect everyone, until the time was right to come clean."

I picked at my nail polish. "He was doing it partly for himself, too. His actions weren't totally selfless."

Mom patted my cheek. "Well, if I met a person like you back then, I would have been a little selfish, too. 'Cause you're pretty darn extraordinary, Jade Abbott."

I blinked at her, waiting for a punch line. "I can't believe this. My mother, Meg Abbott, is defending a guy."

"Not just any guy," she said. "The guy my daughter's fallen for."

I snorted, like she was crazy, but I knew she could see right through me. "What makes you so sure I've fallen for him?"

Mom put her arm around me and we watched travelers buzzing by. "Because you're at an airport, camped outside the security gates for God knows how long now, puffy-eyed and unable to leave."

I sighed, kind of relieved to finally admit it, kind of terrified, too. "Yeah, I know."

"Come on." She stood, pulling me up with her. "Let's get out of here, find something good to eat, and talk."

"Talk about what?"

Mom snagged my duffel from the floor and slung it over her shoulder, leading me away from the security gates. "If you're so unable to leave this place, why don't we go discuss a few things?"

"What kinds of things?" I asked.

"Some life changes I think we should consider."

"Such as?"

"Where you want to spend your senior year of high school," she said with a shrug. "Do we want a house by the beach or one in the hills? Where should we go next summer before you leave for college?"

From the way Mom was glancing over at me, like a kid on Christmas morning, I could guess what she was getting at.

"Don't you have a concert?" I asked.

"Yeah," she said, waving it off. "In twenty-two hours. Plenty of time to answer all of life's questions."

Chapter Nineteen

This had been a summer for the record books. In every way I hadn't planned on.

Mom flew back to Vancouver earlier this morning so she could make her concert, but she'd been right about there being plenty of time to answer life's questions. At least the most pressing ones.

With Uncle Paul and Aunt Julie's help, we were going to find a rental close by for the school year. I'd spend my senior year in an actual school setting, with the same people and the same-ish routine. Aunt Julie had been so stoked about the idea of us being close, she pretty much overlooked my escape to the airport.

There were only a million details to work out, but the plan was in place.

There was only one big thing I still had to work out.

I could just see his bright blue shorts up on the beach ahead, where he crouched beside someone else. His daughter. Lily.

Now that I knew, it was so obvious. I couldn't believe I hadn't figured it out before.

Quentin had plopped Lily on a towel. She was wearing a giant pink sun hat and smacking at the sand with a toy shovel. Even from a ways off I could tell how much sunscreen he'd slathered on her—the girl looked like she'd been practically painted white.

It made me smile, watching them. He was so good with her. I knew most teenage guys probably would have up and run rather than be tied to the responsibilities that came with raising a child alone. He was lucky he had his family, but still, nothing about having a baby was easy, all while you were trying to finish high school and work a part-time job.

No wonder he always looked so tired. No wonder he'd been napping that day in his truck.

It had been so obvious.

Lily let out an excited whoop when Quentin lifted up the turtle sand mold. She looked at the turtle, then up at Quentin as if he was the best thing ever. I knew the feeling.

"She looks just like you, you know that?"

Quentin's back stiffened, but when he turned around, he was smiling. Like he'd been expecting me all along. He patted the sand beside him, getting back to Lily right before she shoved a sand-coated fist into her mouth. "Sorry, kiddo. DNA's a real bummer."

"That was more of a compliment," I said, sitting down beside him.

"Then DNA's the bomb, kid. You can thank me later. You know, when you can actually form words rather than just spit bubbles."

Lily handed a fistful of sand to her dad.

"Hey, Lily. How's it going?" I made a face. She patted the turtle mold with her shovel, looking at me and waiting.

"Fair warning. There's no going back once you make that first sand turtle. I lost count somewhere around nine hundred and fifty." Quentin brushed the sand off his knees. "That's today's tally alone."

I scooped some sand into the mold before pressing it down in front of Lily. An excited whoop, followed by a shovel smack. A half second later, she was blinking at me again, waiting.

"Told ya." He nudged my arm. Both of us stayed quiet as if we were trying to decide how to start this conversation.

Finally, he cleared his throat. "So I can't help but notice you're here. In California." He paused. "You stayed."

I nodded. "Yep."

When Lily tossed a palmful of sand into the air, half of it sprinkled into his hair. He didn't seem to notice. "Why?"

"For a lot of reasons," I said.

"Am I included in those reasons? Maybe?" He sounded unsure, doubtful.

Which made me start to smile. Clearly both of us had been oblivious. Still were.

"Yeah, you are."

He lifted his hand in front of Lily. "Give me some skin."

Lily's shovel high-fived him.

"Mom came here before I could get to her. We talked. A lot." I handed Lily her sippy cup when she motioned at it. "We decided we're going to spend the school year here in California. Once her tour's done, she'll be in the studio, and I'll go to a real school my senior year. We're looking for a house close to my aunt and uncle."

Quentin started grinning. "Does that mean . . ."

"We'll be going to the same school."

That took him a minute to process; then a familiar smirk shifted into place. "Didn't get enough of me this summer?"

I made a face. "Nah. I think there's a whole lot more to get to know."

Quentin grabbed the sippy cup before Lily sent it flying over her shoulder. "Not to disappoint you, but this is my life. Her." He pushed her sun hat down a little farther on her forehead. "What's left after isn't much. You deserve a lot more than that, Jade. You deserve way more than I'll be able to give you."

Another sand turtle met its demise. I already had a new one ready to go. "I think I deserve to be happy." I returned Lily's smile when she sent a toothy grin my way. "And *you* make me happy."

Quentin held out a hand toward me. "You make me happy, too, Jade Abbott." I took his hand without thinking.

"You know, I grew up with only one parent in my life. But the way she loved me was more than having two parents combined." I watched his arm whip out behind Lily when she started to fall back, righting her. He was proving my point that very moment. "Lily's going to turn out just fine. Trust me."

His hand squeezed mine. "I do."

"It wasn't that you had a baby that upset me." I slid closer. "It was that you didn't tell me about her. It wouldn't have been such a big deal, if you'd been the one to tell me."

"I know, but"—he motioned at the diaper bag and baby paraphernalia spread around on the towel—"this isn't an easy life, Jade. For me it's not an option, but for you it is."

I looked over at him. "I don't need easy; I just need real."

"This is as real as it gets, Jade." His eyes found mine. "So if you want to make a run for it, I get it."

I shifted in the sand to get comfortable. He hadn't been joking about the sand turtle thing. "I'm exactly where I want to be."

We sat like that for a while. Not speaking a word but saying everything. He wasn't going anywhere. I wasn't going anywhere. We were both right where we wanted to be.

Acknowledgments

This book was a true labor of love for me. Months after completing Jade and Quentin's story, they're still with me. I guess they always will be. Their story would not be what it is without the team that was committed to giving them the book they deserved.

Endless thanks to my editors, Phoebe Yeh and Elizabeth Stranahan, who poured as much of themselves into *Almost Impossible* as I did. Their insight and feedback were invaluable. Their edits and devotion to this book demonstrate just how committed they are to putting out the best young adult books possible.

Thank you to my agent, Jane Dystel, for her tireless work ethic. I'm grateful to have such a professional, committed agent on my side.

To all the book bloggers who dedicate themselves to spreading the word of books: you all inspire me. To write better. To be better. To *do* better. You give so much to the book world without expecting anything in return. Thank you for continuing to read and share your love of books.

To my Reality Heroines: I hope you all realize just how heroic you truly are. You are my happy online place and I consider you friends, even though I have yet to meet many of you. Thank you for your kindness and unwavering support.

To my husband and daughter: my loves, my life. You are my reasons for everything.

Lastly, to all of you readers out there: thank you for letting this bookworm live her dream. Never settle for anything less than yours.

About the Author

Nicole Williams is the *New York Times* bestselling author of *Crash, Clash,* and *Crush,* and numerous other books, including her first young adult novel, *Trusting You & Other Lies,* which *Booklist* called "a charming summer romance." While never getting to travel the globe at a young age like Jade, Nicole spent her youth imagining all the exotic places she'd go and the adventures she'd have along the way.

Nicole loves reading and writing books about star-crossed lovers and happy endings, but believes some of the best stories are the ones we create every day. Nicole lives with her family in the Evergreen State with her husband and daughter, and they try to travel and find adventure every chance they get. Visit Nicole on Twitter at @nwilliamsbooks, on Facebook, or on her website at authornicolewilliams.com.

Callum promises Phoenix a summer she'll never forget.
But can she trust him . . . or is this just another lie?

Turn the page and fall in love with another
Nicole Williams summer romance!

Excerpt copyright © 2017 by Nicole Williams. Published by Crown Books
for Young Readers, an imprint of Random House Children's Books,
a division of Penguin Random House LLC, New York.

ONE

For the one thousandth time, I shifted in the backseat, trying to get more comfortable, but I should have known better. Nothing about this summer was going to be comfortable, not even the leather seat that was supposed to be all ergonomic and crap—making road trips a dream, my dad had claimed. After doing almost six hours of hard time in the backseat, I could confidently say that my dad's definitions of *dream* and *nightmare* had gotten crossed.

The air-conditioning inside the Ainsworth family Range Rover was blasting from the front seat, where my parental units sat, but they might as well have been on opposite poles of the planet for as much as they'd acknowledged each other on this four-hundred-mile-and-some-change road trip.

I adjusted my seat-heat, dialing it up a notch when I noticed my mom crank up the air-conditioning from frosty to arctic. A faint sigh slipped past her lips as she angled the vents toward her face. Any other human being would have been sprouting icicles out their nose from the way that glacial air was blasting at her, but instead she continued to fan her face, like it was still too warm.

The leggings and tunic I'd thrown on were not holding up to the cold front, so I snagged my North Shore Track & Field hoodie from my backpack. I pulled up the hood and tied the drawstring around my face. Despite the sweatshirt, a shiver rocked me right before the seat-heat started to do its job. My mom might have been born and raised in the Northeast, but I was Californian born and bred. I didn't do below sixty degrees unless I was sporting a couple extra layers.

"We're almost there." Dad pointed at a sign on the side of the road, but I couldn't have read it if I'd wanted to. We'd been hauling ass ever since he'd pulled out of our driveway in Santa Monica.

"Still looking through that brochure?" Dad glanced back at Harrison, my ten-year-old little brother, who was sitting beside me and thumbing through the camp brochure I knew he'd memorized fifty flip-throughs ago.

Harrison, or Harry as I called him despite my mom's protests that the nickname was much too "ordinary," scooted his glasses higher on his nose.

"Fencing's that thing where they wear the weird masks and dance around each other, right?" Harry asked.

"That's right. It's kind of like medieval sword-fighting, but with blunted swords that won't totally maim or injure the opponent." Dad glanced at Harry again, which made me all kinds of uneasy given he was speeding into a sharp corner going at least fifty miles per hour.

"That sounds sick!" Harry pulled a pink highlighter from his side pocket and drew a surprisingly straight line over *Fencing* under the activities section of the brochure. Most of the few dozen others were already highlighted. Everything besides basket-weaving, papier-mâché, and cake decorating were highlighted in different colors depending on Harry's level of interest.

He had a key for it and everything. A yellow highlighter meant he was interested, a green one meant he was *very* interested, an orange one meant he'd be camped out the night before so he could be first in line, and a pink one meant he'd sacrifice a litter of puppies to do it. For a kid whose life had consisted of textbooks, music lessons, and computers, this was the adventure of a lifetime—almost as major as winning a lottery to go to the moon.

For someone like me, though? A teen girl who'd planned to spend her last official summer at the beach, playing volleyball during the day and huddling around bonfires at night before going away to college next fall—this was like serving a life sentence in a maximum security prison, the guards being my parents, my cell being some "rustic" cabin smack in the middle of nowhere.

I wanted to spend the summer before my senior year at Camp KissMyButt in Flagstaff, Arizona, about as much as I wanted to be locked in the same bedroom where I'd found my former boyfriend rounding second base with my former friend at a party a few weeks ago. Keats—former boyfriend, current buttmunch—had blamed it on his overconsumption of tequila that night. I'd blamed it on his underconsumption of self-control over his whole life.

Whoever was right, the outcome was the same. We were done. Through. Good-bye and good riddance.

That was my mantra, though my conviction lagged sometimes.

"Sick, sick, *sick,*" Harry said as he continued to devour the camp brochure.

"Harrison, please stop talking like you're auditioning for a rap video." My mom's eyes were closed, like they'd been the majority of the trip, but now she was pressing her temples, which meant a headache was coming on. She'd had headaches for as long as I could remember. She blamed them on the California sun and not being used to so much sunshine, even after two decades of living beneath it. Lately, her headaches had been a lot more frequent. The sun wasn't to blame for the majority of them now, though.

"Sorry, Mom." After drawing another wide pink line through *Fencing*, Harry added a few exclamation points on either side of the word. "Fencing sounds both mentally and physically stimulating." Harry smiled up at her, but she didn't see it.

Harry was Mom's little clone, her shadow for the first five years of his life, and the child she deemed worthy of living vicariously through. I'd always been more of my dad's carbon copy and used to love knowing I'd gotten all my drive and ambition from him.

I didn't feel that way anymore.

"So? Can I do it?" Harry flipped to the last page of the brochure.

Mom twisted around in her seat just enough so that she could look at us when she opened her eyes.

Harry took after our mom in the looks department—fair skin, dark hair, slight build—but everyone said I had her eyes. That had been a point of pride, but then things changed. The person who used to be my mom seemed to have disappeared, and I wasn't so sure I wanted the same eyes as the person sitting in the front seat now.

Before Mom glanced my way, I made sure I'd angled my body as far as I could toward the door and stared out the window like the sight of pine trees and blue skies was killin' it on the first Saturday of summer break. The same day when all my friends were getting together at Laguna Beach to kick off the first beach party of the summer. I'd had my headphones on the entire trip, too, but I'd only listened to music from home to the Arizona state line. I'd kept them on the rest of the way, though, because they spared me whatever awkward talks my parents had in mind for this trip.

"Can you do what, Harrison?" Mom asked when her eyes wandered his way.

"Fencing." He shrugged.

Mom's forehead creased into several deep wrinkles as her mouth drew a hard line. "I don't know if that's a good idea. What about pottery? Or cake decorating? Don't those sound like compelling options?"

Harry looked at our mom like she'd just suggested he slip into lederhosen and take up yodeling, but she didn't see it. She'd already twisted around in her seat and squeezed her eyes shut as she massaged her temples.

Harry crossed his arms and put on the face Dad made when he wasn't happy. "I don't want to spend my whole summer learning how to bake. Or make stupid pots. We're going to one of the most adventure-filled places in the country." Harry thrust his hand against the front of the brochure, where, I guessed, he was reading one of the quotes. "I want to fence, and mountain bike, and fish, and climb a rock face—"

"Climb a rock face?" Really, if she rubbed at her temples any harder, she was going to give herself brain damage. "I don't think so, Harrison. Be reasonable."

It was really hard to keep the listening-to-music act up and stay quiet. Who told a ten-year-old boy to be reasonable? Who actually expected they were capable of it?

Beside me, Harry slumped in his seat. The brochure fell onto his lap as he stuffed the highlighter in his pocket.

"Hey, we'll see. Okay? Let's take it one day at a time. No need to leap right in." Dad reached his long arm out and patted

Harry on the knee a few times, like that was all it would take to make a kid feel better after crushing his summer vacation dreams.

I had to shift in my seat and bite the inside of my cheek to keep my mouth shut. My parents could mess each other up all they wanted if that was what they were into, but when it came to dragging Harry into their three-ring circus, I got a little touchy. Last time I'd gotten a "little touchy," I'd lost cell phone privileges for two weeks.

I distracted myself with my phone. I'd played enough games on the trip so far to qualify for gamer status, so I decided to do a quick drive-by of the social media scene. My dad had assured me there was Wi-Fi and cell reception up here at this Camp BlowsBigTime, but I wasn't going to take his word for it. Dad's word wasn't exactly golden these days. I'd caught him in so many lies I'd stopped counting.

This might be my last chance to check in with friends and make a few final words before dying to the world for the next couple of months.

I replied to a few friends' comments and posts, trying to distract myself from why I'd really logged on—to check Keats's profile picture. It was still the same—the photo of the two of us staring at that sunset like we'd figured out a way to freeze time. When I found myself relaxing into my seat, a smile starting to form, I dropped my phone in my lap and cursed under my breath.

That guy was not worth smiling over ever again.

My phone buzzed against my thigh. When I turned it over, I saw it was a text from my best friend, Emerson. You're not thinking about him are you?

I cursed under my breath again. The girl claimed she had psychic powers—I was a believer. *Thinking of who?*

Emerson had never been Team Keats for no other reason than believing that dating such a good-looking guy who was also fully aware of it was like handing my heart over to a rugby team to use for practice. I'd defended him, saying he couldn't help it if girls fell over themselves to brush his shoulder passing in the hallway. They could keep right on loitering at his locker and sliding into the seat beside him in class—he wasn't open for business.

Turned out, I'd been in serious denial, as I'd discovered the night I found my "closed for business" boyfriend getting it on with "her" a couple of clothing pieces away from moving on to the next stage. What sucked even more was that the girl I'd caught rubbing crotches with my boyfriend wasn't the kind of girl you'd automatically think would be the boyfriend-hunter type. She was on the track team with me, got good grades, and was well liked and respected by the male and female populations of North Shore. It would have made it easier to hate them both if she had a reputation of low standards and zero class. But she didn't. And neither did Keats.

Of course, realizing that made me do what any other teenage girl would—I spent the next week and a half analyzing what the hell had happened. Was it me? Was it her? Was it him? Was it something she had that I didn't? Was it something he felt for her that he didn't for me? Was it because I'd held out for so long that a certain part of Keats's anatomy had finally fallen off like he'd predicted it would if we waited much longer? If overthinking a situation became a high school sport, I'd be the captain of that team, too, and lead it to another state championship.

"Her" had a name, of course, but it was one I'd never speak again. Get caught kissing a good friend's boyfriend? Yeah, that landed you smack in you're-dead-to-me territory.

Good girl was Emerson's reply, immediately followed by *BTW, summer sucks without you.*

As a new policy I'd adopted a few months ago, I made it a point not to smile when my parents were around. I didn't want them to get the wrong idea that I was happy being in their presence, and I sure as hell didn't want them thinking I was thrilled with the sudden detour in my summer vacation plans. I occasionally set that no-smiling policy aside when Harry was close by, though. I didn't want to take it out on him when I was mad at them.

I might have let a smile slip when I read Emerson's text, though.

Summer sucks without you too, I typed, holding my breath when it took a few extra moments to send. We were winding higher and steeper up the gravel road, which only looked wide enough for one car, making me wonder if there was another way down. If there was, I'd find it. I'd use it, too. I was four months from being eighteen—an adult in the eyes of the law—and my parents were treating me like a kid in dragging me up here.

Emerson's text vibrated in my hand. **How's the fam?**

I scanned the inside of the car and frowned. *How do you think?*

Things have to get better soon.

I wiggled further down in my seat. *They couldn't get worse.*

Emerson's reply came about five seconds later. She made other text-savvy teens look like amateurs. **Have you talked to them about you know what?**

My knuckles went white from the fists I was making. I practically had to pry my fingers open to text her back. *No. Not sure how to work that into a conversation.*

How about . . . Hey Dad and Mom, about that eviction notice I found under that stack of unpaid bills.

I swallowed as I punched in my reply. *Ugh. I'd rather be in denial over it like they are.*

I glanced over at Harry. He'd flopped his head against the headrest and closed his eyes. When Dad glanced in the rearview mirror, I accidentally caught his gaze. I got back to admiring the ocean of trees and tried not to make a face. I was already sick of trees. And I was expected to spend ten weeks surrounded by them and not go insane? The ozone had a better chance of repairing itself with a hot glue gun and a roll of plastic wrap.

My phone vibrated with Emerson's text. You should talk to them about it.

My foot started bouncing. *They should talk to me about it.*

Fine. Someone should talk to someone about it.

I didn't text anything back right away. I was too busy distracting myself from throwing my fist through the window. Dad had lost his job two years ago, and I got how tough that must have been for him, but instead of picking himself up and dusting himself off, he decided to let it snowball out of control. He still hadn't found a new job, money was running out, he and Mom only communicated in glares and shouts, and now there was an eviction notice.

He'd lost his job, but you would have thought he'd lost everything else as well from the way he'd been acting. Mom too. Once upon a time he'd been like a hero to me. Now he barely played a walk-on role in my life.

The only reason we were able to afford this vacation was because the guy who owned the cabin was an old friend of my dad's. He'd given us some kind of friend discount, which I later discovered meant a total discount. As in, we were getting to stay for free. Our cabin was older and didn't get rented out anymore, but I didn't enjoy feeling like a charity case.

So, yeah. Trust issues. I had them. Big-time. Side effect of the most important people in your life lying to you.

Beside me, Harry gave the faintest of moans. Of course I was the only one who'd noticed. "Hey." I gave his knee a soft squeeze. "You okay?"

Keeping his eyes clamped closed, he nodded.

I noticed Harry shifting in his seat, like he couldn't get comfortable. His face was starting to turn a familiar shade of green as his hand went to cover his mouth. I'd seen this enough times to know what was happening.

"Dad, pull over." I leaned across Harry's lap and punched one of the half-dozen buttons on the door's armrest. Harry's window whirred down, letting in a blast of fresh air. For summer in Arizona, the air was surprisingly cool. I was expecting it to be blistering hot and the air to smell like BO. This was almost refreshing.

"Hello? Calling all parental figures." I snapped my fingers next to Dad's ear. "Puke coming. Pull over."

Of course that would get his attention. Dad loved this car. It wasn't even his, and it wouldn't be his when the lease was up because he couldn't afford to buy it or anything like it. He wouldn't even be able to scrounge up enough money or credit to buy one of those domestic four-doors in the used car lots he cringed at as he drove by.

"Need me to pull over, Harry?"

Harry shook his head, angling his nose so the fresh air was streaming straight into it. "No. Keep going. I'll be okay."

"Harry," I urged, knowing what he was up to. He was trying to be tough. He wanted our parents to stop treating him like he was a piece of ancient family china that needed to be handled with the utmost care. To him, pulling over would be a defeat. Sucking it up and keeping his breakfast down was a win in his book.

That was messed up in my book.

"Harrison?" Mom chimed in.

"Harry?" The first thing Dad's eyes went to was the light beige carpet at Harry's feet. *Yeah, that's right, Dad. Worry about the carpet in the car instead of your kid whose stomach was unleashing on him. Way to have your priorities straight.*

"I'm *fine*. Just keep going," Harry whined, curling into a ball.

Dad's gaze went back to the carpet at Harry's feet before he punched the gas, because we weren't moving fast enough at fifty.

Harry was in crisis mode. He was desperate to prove to our parents that he was strong and capable of more than just wiping his own ass and tying his shoes. This was his summer. Since this clearly wasn't going to be mine, I had all the time in the world to help him with his agenda.

"Here, this will help. . . ." Twisting around in my seat, I dug through the stuffed third-row seat for the mini cooler I'd packed with essentials like Junior Mints, Red Vines, soda, and . . . There it was. I pulled the mini ice pack from the cooler and pressed it to the back of Harry's neck.

Harry had been prone to car sickness since the day he left the hospital and yacked all over his coming-home outfit. I didn't know why I was the only one who seemed to notice that any time he was stuffed in a car for longer than an hour his stomach staged a revolt, but it would have to remain a mystery. I'd stopped asking questions like that when I realized there weren't any answers. At least no good ones.

A moment later, I reached into the cooler to pull a Sprite free. I cracked it open, and an eruption of fizz and tiny bubbles floated into my face. "Drink this. Car sickness won't stand a chance against the ice pack–Sprite tag team."

Harry's breath was already returning to normal when he

took the frosty can of pop from me. I wrapped my hand around the ice pack and pressed it more firmly on his neck. "Better?"

He took a sip, then followed it up with a relieved sigh. "So much." He took another sip, then opened his eyes. He smiled at me and, abandoning my no-smiles-allowed policy when our parents were around, I smiled, too. "Thanks, Phoenix. Thanks for always having my back."

My smile crept higher. Part of Harry's quest to become his own ten-year-old man was picking up a few choice words and phrases he'd heard from my friends. *Sick* and *having my back* were two of the many. There were a couple of others I'd had to bribe him to forget. "Thanks for always having mine."

He extended his fist toward me. I bumped it with mine and winked. The Ainsworth family's one redeeming quality was my brother. How this little ball of optimism and loyalty could have been spawned from my parents was the eighth wonder of the world.

If there was one reason to not start exploring escape options the moment I set foot in Camp GatesOfHell, it was so I wouldn't abandon my little brother with two people bent on driving their own lives off a cliff.

I checked Harry over again. His skin was normal, along with his breathing. Crisis averted.

"Tell Emerson hey for me." He glanced at my phone and chugged the last of his Sprite before unleashing a burp that would not end.

"Harrison . . . ," Mom warned in *that* tone. The one that basically implied she and her kind didn't burp, fart, poop, or pick boogers.

"Sorry, Mom," he said, grinning at me like he'd just gotten away with stealing an armored truck's worth of *Minecraft* games and ice cream sandwiches.

I'd tilted my phone just enough so Harry could read Emerson's name at the top. He loved Emerson. As in wanted to marry her. He had good taste in girls—I had to give him that—and she was just crazy enough she might actually consider it one day.

"We're here," Dad announced, finally easing off the gas as we passed under a gleaming wood sign hanging between two more—big surprise—trees. No more trees. For the love of God. This wasn't natural.

CAMP KISMET was carved in big letters that looked as if a kid wielding a melon baller had done it. I hadn't been too far off with the *Camp KissMyButt* name.

Harry's face was hanging out the window, taking it all in, pointing at so many things his arm was a blur. Dad rolled down his window and hung his elbow out. Even Mom had opened her eyes and stopped drilling at her temples long enough to inspect the approaching camp.

Me, though? No way. Slumping down further into my seat, I plunked my dark sunglasses into place, put one of the songs we played at track meets on repeat, jacked up the volume, and sent another text to Emerson. *I hate my life.*

Of course that was when I went from three bars to no bars, trapping her reply in no-reception limbo.

"This is going to be the best summer ever!" Harry shouted as log cabins came into view. Great. I'd be spending my summer learning about how the pioneers had lived back in the day.

Crossing my arms, I slumped as low as I could into the seat. I wasn't holding my breath for this to be the best summer ever—I was crossing my fingers, hoping it wouldn't be the worst.